SEAL Team Seven
Logan
By
Jordan Silver

Table of Contents

Chapter 1

LOGAN

"Babe, move that ass faster I'm close, stop fucking around." I had to grit my teeth to keep from shooting too soon. I even smacked her ass to get her going, but she was in one of her moods.

My poor boy was hanging on for dear life, we'd both grown accustomed to her trying to one-up our ass, but I'm all man so she's never gonna win this fight. She's playing dirty this morning though, the little sneak.

She kept teasing me, moving her hips around and around in circles, then lifting up slowly, before dropping down hard on my cock. The sensations were unbelievable as my cock pushed up into her.

Looking up at her as she pulled on her nipples, head thrown back, her flat stomach concaved as she rode me for her own pleasure, I grabbed her hips and tried moving her the way I needed so I could cum.

She's been teasing me for a good half an hour now and I had no doubt it was to get back at me for the torture I put her through when I ate her sweet pussy for an hour. No good deed and all that happy shit.

"Gabriella, fuck, now." She clenched down on my dick so that no matter how much I tried pulling and pushing it made no difference, that's her new trick.

"I've got something for your ass love of mine." I loved being in her like this first thing in the morning. With the birds chirping right outside the window, the sun, trying to make its presence known, and all else was still. It's part of our routine, one I hoped to have for the next sixty years at least.

She rolled over this morning, with a smile on her face, probably remembering the pounding I'd given her the night before. That's all it took for me to pounce. Now I was buried balls-deep as she tickled the head of my cock with her cervix.

On her last downward plunge I slammed into her hard. Her mouth and eyes flew open and already she was bathing my cockhead with her sweet juices. My baby likes her man to do her rough on occasion for all that she's a dainty little thing. I lucked the fuck out there for sure. A fucker like me needs a little raw in the mornings.

Before she could react to my assault on her pussy I switched us over, placing her beneath me with her legs caught in the crook of my arms. She was open to me as I bored into her deeper her sweet cries ringing out in the early morning hours. "Shit Logan wait a minute."

"Uh uh, you had your chance." I showed her no mercy as I fucked into her hard and deep, her pussy wrapped tightly around my cock as it sawed in and out of her.

"You wanna play, huh?" I looked down between us at where my twelve and a half inch rod pinned her to the bed with each thrust. That shit looked massive. I kept my eyes locked there as I started to fuck. In, out in out, side to side, before burying my dick to the hilt in her heated pussy.

She wailed and threw her legs around as her pussy sucked at me, like she was trying to get even my nut sac in there.

"You close babydoll?" Fuck, be close greedy my dick is too happy to keep this shit up much longer. "Yes almost there." Her voice was breathless as her hips met mine, her ass bouncing off the bed from the hard pounding I was giving her. My kinda sex.

"Fuck I'm there cum with me." I took her nipple between my lips and sucked hard knowing that that was one of her triggers. When I felt the liquid heat of her pussy juices covering me once again, I let go and emptied deep inside her. I felt my balls drain out inside her down to the last drop, as she twitched and sighed beneath me.

I took a moment lying on top of her, pulling her body in close, before dropping to the side and pulling her over on top of me. My girl likes to cuddle after sex so I have to give her what she wants, even though I'm already running late and it's her fault for teasing the shit out of me.

I laid there for a good ten minutes while she ran her hands all over my chest and arms. She was riding the last bit of steel out of my cock like she wasn't quite finished with me yet. Much more of this shit and my rod will be up and ready to go again. She doesn't listen for shit.

"You done?"

"Maybe, why?" She did that cat in heat thing that these southern belle types have down to a fine art.

"Why, because I'm supposed to be somewhere ten minutes ago and if I'm not off this bed in the next five there's a good chance my nosy ass brothers are gonna bust down the door and come looking."

That didn't seem to register too well since she was still doing the bump and grind on my dick. "But I like feeling you inside me." She squeezed around my cock, trying to get a rise out of him.

"Fine, I'm going to do you one last time but then I've gotta go." I pulled out and used my fist to wipe our mixed juices off my rod. "Suck me back to hard and I'll take care of your pussy, but then I've got to go." She was only too happy to get on her knees in the middle of the bed and take my meat into her mouth, totally ignoring my stern look. A little more than a month ago she'd been a virgin; that was a thing of the past. In that time she's tried to get me to teach her everything there is to know about sex. When I wasn't working at the site or running ops with the guys for our upcoming mission, I was riding between her legs.

"You remember what I showed you?" I wrapped her long golden locks around my fist as she moved her head up and down on my meat. "Uh-huh." She opened her mouth wider and prepared to suck me the way I liked.

"Well do it." I hit the back of her throat on my next stroke in and her eyes came up to meet mine. I could see the bulge of my cock in her neck with each fuck I took into her mouth, and her spit and my per-cum was starting to run down her chin.

"Do you want the bed or the floor babydoll?" It took her a minute to ease off my tool so she could answer. "Why, what's the difference?" I played with her chin as she looked up at me with innocent eyes. How could she be such an enigma? "The bed will get you a nice slow fuck, the floor will get you hard and fast, choose one."

She hopped off the bed and landed on the floor next to it on her hands and knees, with her ass in the air, and the pink of her pussy winking at me from between her thighs.

"That's my girl." I led with my dick as I got off and went to stand behind her. I used the thick head of my cock to tease her from clit to slit while she hissed and threw her ass back at me, looking for dick.

I smacked her ass cheek once with the flat of my heavy cock before giving in and sinking into her. She arched her back and hissed when I hit bottom, her legs spreading wider, to take me in deep. "Oh yeah, you're feeling nasty." I planted my feet firmly and bent my knees as I drilled into her pussy, going deep.

"Yes, oh please Logan, do it." I know what she meant, what she craved. If the good people of our little town ever found out that one of their daughters was as wild as this one they'd never believe it.

I pulled her hair back roughly as I surged into her pussy, using her hair like a horse's mane to pull her on and off my rod. As promised it was hard, quick and just a little rough.

It wasn't long before I was emptying my seed in her belly again while she creamed my cock and wailed like I was killing her ass. I kept sliding in and out of her even though we'd both got off, as my dick dripped inside her.

I've been playing it loose and fancy free in her pussy since I took her cherry. There was no threat of disease and the question of breeding her was of no consequence since she'd practically booked the wedding hall. As far as she was concerned we were already hitched, so who was I to argue? I dripped the last few drops of cum inside her before pulling her head back so we could share one last kiss before we both headed for the shower.

"What's on the agenda for today babydoll?" She gave me a run down of what her day looked like. Now this was not idle chatter bullshit, I seriously paid attention to where she was going and whatnot because of what was going on in the town, things that she knew nothing about.

I didn't want her going into any dangerous situations. I signed off on her plans, which was mostly wedding shit.

I lathered up my hands and washed her body as she stood in front of me. Her body was truly a thing of artistic beauty. High firm tits that were the perfect D cup with the sexiest penny sized nipples, a slender waist that flared off into her hips and a nice fat ass. Her crowning glory is her wild mane of multi colored hair that makes her bottle green eyes just light up.

At twenty-five she's seven years younger than me. Some thought maybe too young and innocent to deal with a man like me, who led the life I did. I really didn't give a fuck what some thought; she was mine.

I'd seen her wanted her and made it happen. The fears of her family were well understood, I am after all an unknown, ex military and I ride a bike to boot with my brothers, which some people automatically perceives as a biker crew, and we all know the reputations bikers have.

As far as they are concerned, the daughter of a prominent businessman had no right being caught up in my world. Their arguments might've worked if she hadn't fallen as hard for me as I had her.

One look and we were both hooked and nothing and no one had been able to stand in our way. Her old man had tried paying me off; he'd almost lost his life for that insult. I still had that shit on video; I'm keeping it for kicks and giggles.

I had of course shown it to her the same day. My little tigress had lit into her dad and moved out of his house an hour later, and straight into my bed. It helped that she was best friends with my new little sister Danielle, my brother Connor's fiancée.

In fact it was because of Dani that we had even met. Like I said, it was lust at first sight, and in spite of my asshole brothers' ribbing, that lust had morphed into something more almost overnight.

With Gabriella it was like being side swiped with a semi truck. There was no real warning, just wham, out of nowhere and I was blindsided. It happened so easily and without much fanfare, that I didn't even know what the fuck had hit me. I think I was thinking the way I always did; I'd hit it and be done in a couple weeks more or less, but one look, one taste and here we are. I knew from fuck one that I was in trouble.

Chapter 2

LOGAN

I hadn't wasted any time getting her into my bed and that's where she's been ever since. The girls keep each other busy when the boys and I are out on patrol, and they both have work during the day. Something I was coming to terms with, since if I had my way, she'd never leave the safety of the compound. Not without me, or one of my brothers riding rough shod anyway.

Her job was pretty much like Dani's something I noticed about this side of the country. People were big on having their kids come work with them or for them or whatever the fuck. Unlike Dani though, this one was the company's buyer or some shit, and this branch dealt in high-end art deals among other things. I can hold a conversation about that shit for about ten minutes before my ears, eyes and every fuck else starts to bleed, so it's good that we have other interest.

So far we'd blended pretty well together, she knew my position on most things, which boiled down to I'm the man, you do what I say and everyone's safe that way. She does have random moments of female crazy when she thinks she can do her own thing and get away with it.

I guess that stems from being raised by parents who thought giving their kid her way in everything was the way to go. With me she's on a tight leash. I think that was one of the things that soured her dad against me in the beginning.

He didn't like that I called the shots. Or more to the point, that his little girl got off on that shit and was only to happy to obey her man.

Men who call the shots have been given a bad reputation in the last few years. That's because some assholes have abused the privilege, but I'm not about to put my woman's life in danger because society was too fuck stupid to know the difference between a man who gave a fuck and an abuser.

I've seen the underbelly of mankind when I was in the trenches. Society can get fucked; I'm tagging her ass from the get. Wherever she goes, I'm gonna know, not because I wanna control her, but because I wanna keep every other motherfucker out there with an agenda away from what's mine, and keep her ass safe at the same time.

Her dad is one of those who don't know the difference, either that or he thinks that's his role and had a hard time relinquishing that shit to someone else, especially someone like yours truly. I'm sure I'm nobody's ideal of their little girl's prince charming; I could give a fuck and told him so in no uncertain terms. If he or anyone else in this town thought I was giving her up because of their fucked up prejudices, they were out their fucking minds.

Things were a little more civil between us these days. I guess a couple of weeks without any contact had been too much for her mother and she had put her foot down. My girl had stood her ground, if her dad didn't apologize to me she would never step foot back in their home again. What she didn't understand was I hadn't punched her father in the face because he'd insulted me, but because of the insult to her.

She was priceless as far as I was concerned and her happiness meant more to me than anything else. If I'd thought for one second that me being in her life wasn't good for her, I loved her enough that I would've walked away, okay that's a fucking lie but whatever. I admit to a shitload of selfishness on my part, Gabriella is the best thing that has ever happened to me, no one or nothing had ever given me that feeling of completeness I get when I am with her, there was no way I was giving that up, not for anything.

I'd given my blood for my country, why the fuck didn't I deserve one of the best it had to offer? Meanwhile I hadn't been looking for her, but that didn't stop me from going all in.

Not even the unmerciful teasing I'd had to endure from my brothers had swayed me; I was locked in there for good. The thought didn't even scare me anymore, not like it did in the beginning when all I could think is 'what the blue fuck?'

The fact that she loved me made life a hell of a lot more bearable than it had been before. I didn't have the best of childhoods, my mother was a truck stop waitress, who got knocked up by a trucker, who used to come through town and sell her dreams. Until the day she told him she was pregnant and she never laid eyes on him again. As a kid, I spent lots of time alone. Being raised in a small- town, people didn't follow the same tenets as big city dwellers.

No one thought too much about a young single mom leaving her five-year old son alone while she went out to make a living during the summer months when school was out. That kid learned a lot about the streets at an early age.

The old guys who hung around at the local bar didn't have any problem teaching him the facts of life. When most kids my age was learning to read and write, I was learning the ins and outs of a hard knock life.

Mom did the best she could I don't hold anything against the old girl. In fact, after I started making real money a few years ago, I'd set her up in a nice little house in the middle of town. It had always been her dream, the white picket fence, and the little flower garden. I made sure she had everything she'd ever wanted, including a cruise every year for her birthday for her and one of her girlfriends. She didn't need to work anymore if she didn't want to, but she liked to always be doing stuff, so she'd taken up sewing, and now had a nice little business.

Some of my old mentors had passed on a lot of knowledge. The less hardcore had taught me that an education was the best escape from Thomasville. The thing is, I never wanted to escape my town, I loved the picturesque small town with the Rockies as a backdrop; no I wanted to escape poverty.

I went into the service where I met my brothers and the commander, which led me here to another small town on the other side of the country, and her, my fucking life.

My brothers and I had our shit together, I made sure of that. And with the inheritance from the commander, we were pretty much set. All that was missing for each of us was a good woman. My brother Connor had found his with my new little sister Danielle and I was pretty sure the others won't be far behind, no matter how much they bitched and moaned.

The only fly in my ointment was the illegal activities that seemed to be plaguing our little slice of heaven. That, and the fact that pretty soon I was gonna have to leave and go take care of something for Uncle Sam, the fuck.

When she was through prattling away at me about everything under the sun, we had a rushed breakfast together. Being in the service had taught me a lot of disciplines and structure and shit, so I was big on doing things a certain way.

Not that I was regimented or anything like that, but I believed having some kind of routine between us would work, so breakfast together in the mornings and dinner at night was a must. We fucked around the clock so I had no fear of shit going dry there. If I hadn't been running late, we would've been at whomever's turn it was to cook this morning, another one of our traditions I aim to keep.

"I want you home before dark and don't let the sunset catch you in the other town you hear me?" I was expecting an argument, she argues me to death about everything, and sometimes I let her, if it's not a big deal, other times, like now, all it takes is a look.

"But Logan we have so much to do. I know to a man it might not seem like much, but planning a wedding is not a nine to five operation." I guess my silence alerted her to the danger she was about to walk her ass right into. I'd told her about that shit, but things were still new and it looked like it was gonna take her some more time yet, to get the hang of this shit.

She looked up from her bowl of fruit and caught the look on my face, nothing sinister, just a raised brow; but that was enough to have her backtracking and acting like she had some damn sense. "Fine, I'll be home before dark."

"The fuck is it that y'all got to do today anyway, build the damn hall?" "Very funny Logan, I will have you know, we're looking at patterns for the tables and chairs, we still haven't chosen the crystal…"

Her mouth was moving but I wasn't hearing shit. I held my hand up for her to stop. "Sorry I asked." Was Connor really getting involved in this shit? I have got to have a word with my brother; this was some female shit, and no place for warriors.

"I know that look Logan and you promised so don't even."

"The fuck did I promise?" I drank the last of my coffee and rose to leave before she talked me into some shit I was not even interested in, she's good at that shit. Usually she waits 'til I'm inside her to start her shit, but if she's pulling her stunts at the damn breakfast table that means I've been slipping.

"You said we could discuss this stuff and you'd help but so far you always come up with excuses..."

"Uh huh and when did we have this conversation about me having anything to do with this shit, or more to the point, handing over my balls? Just book the church, put on a dress and let's do this shit already." I knew she was gonna have something to say about that, and was in no way surprised by the loud screech. My baby can make some annoying ass noises when she wants to.

I put my shit in the dishwasher and tried to make my escape before she wound down. If that bottom lip of hers starts to tremble she can talk me into pretty much anything, so I needed to be out of dodge in case that shit was next on her agenda. "But Logan…"

"Ehhhh, gotta go to work baby." I kept my eyes forward as I held up my hand for silence and beat feet for the door. Fucking sly ass female, she sped up behind me and I moved faster, it was a bitch move but what the fuck was I supposed to do?

The woman was driving me crazy with this shit. Connor was looking like he was weakening on this front and I'd be fucked if I'm gonna be knee deep in tulle and flowers and whatever the fuck else she's always lecturing me about when it comes to the wedding.

That shit'll just be fodder for Ty and his smartass mouth, and I really didn't want to have to off one of my brothers over this shit. But if he called me bitch made one more time because of this wedding shit, I'm gonna have to cap him.

Chapter 3

LOGAN

"You fucks ready let's roll." They were lined off like sentinels outside in my yard waiting for me. I ignored their disrespectful smirks and grabbed the cup of coffee Connor held out to me. It was his turn for breakfast again I guess, then again since he'd brought Dani home I don't think any of the others had seriously taken up cooking duty again.

It was sexist I know, but I preferred a good home cooked meal prepared by someone who knew what the fuck they were doing, to a half ass job by one of my brothers. The bra burners could go fuck themselves. Gabriella was shy about cooking for them for some reason, but I wasn't about to push her, she'd come around when she was ready or the fucks could eat take out when it was our turn.

"We were waiting for you bro damn, it's getting harder and harder to get a move on these days. Those of us who aren't leg shackled would like to get the day started at a decent hour you know."

Quinn was always the other one starting some shit. It's like he and Tyler took turns being the assholes of the bunch. I took a sip of hickory and headed for my bike.
"Fuck you Quinn." The laughter that followed brought a smile to my face. Things had been kind of tense since we'd got the orders that were still up in the air.

We were all just getting into the groove of things here and no one was looking forward to heading back into the deep dark hole that was this war. Especially since we'd already fought this particular fight once before; it smacked of repetition.

Not to mention it was extremely rare to be given a heads-up about an upcoming mission like this one. Usually an order came in and you had to be out in the next five minutes, no questions.

I wasn't too thrilled about that and I'm sure my brothers were probably starting to think along the same lines, but we were all waiting to see which way the wind blows. If anything looks too hinky to me I'd scratch the fuck no questions, I wasn't about to walk my team into some fucked up situation that some asshole in a higher position pulled together out his ass.

It's been known to happen more than the American public may know. That's what happens when assholes start using the armed men and women of the nation as their own personal mercs, evil, twisted fucks.

On top of that we'd made some moves that could set things off here in our own backyard, and we were waiting to see the results from that. After much deliberation we'd gone ahead and moved the laundered money that someone had put in Danielle's name through her family's charity. Robert her ex was still insisting that he didn't know who he was working for and Crampton had given up all he had. Whoever was pulling their strings was still in the shadows, which was a dangerous thing for all involved; it was like chasing smoke.

Our stakeouts down at the pier still hadn't given up anything and the old guys weren't having any luck either. It's as if whoever we were dealing with had eyes and ears all around and knew when to lay low.

I didn't like that theory, it spoke volumes as to what we might be dealing with here and that wasn't good. I guess we could've called in local law enforcement by now, but what were we gonna tell them? And besides, we're not big on trusting that shit. More often than not those fuckers were on the take. How else can you explain an operation that was so well insulated? Nah, I'll hold off on that for now

***

We rode out in formation, some of us on our bikes and some in trucks, according to what role we were gonna play today. Sometimes someone had to make a supply run or some shit, so a bike wasn't gonna cut it. I could see why the people here were still getting used to us we were a militant a little bunch to be sure. Even the way we rode shouted military, do not fuck with us. Add the tats and shit and well you had blueprint for stereotyping.

Quinn and Ty were fucking with Connor in his truck, tailgating him like fucking teenagers as they left through the gate. I waited for the others to pull out ahead of me as I sat my ride. I always ride in the back just in case some shit is about to go down. Cowards hardly ever come at you straight on, so I knew whatever popped off would more than likely come from the rear. I wasn't expecting shit to go there in this little town, but I was trained to prepare for anything, and never let them catch you slipping.

My phone rang just as I turned the key in the ignition. I didn't check the readout because I thought it was my woman. She likes to call and fill my ear with cutesy shit to start my day off, even though I'd just left her body not an hour ago.

"Hey." I was already smiling like a sap.
"Do you know what your commander was up to before he died?"

"Say what?"

"You should really look into that before you go digging into things that don't have anything to do with you. Some of us don't appreciate nosy fuckers messing around in our business." The line went dead. I slammed out of the truck with my hand up in the command position. I was sure they could all see me since we hadn't cleared the fucking property yet.

To a man they all stopped and came towards me, faces already set in stern lines because they knew some shit had gone down. I waited until they were all within spitting distance so my words wouldn't carry.

"Just got a call, don't know who yet, but listen." I'd hit record on my phone as soon as the robotic voice had started talking. The same message replayed and my brothers already had their backs up before it was over.

"That's bullshit."

"Of course it is Connor, we know that. But this hump is obviously up to something. We gotta think, why would they go to all this trouble, for what? Did you hear him say 'nosy fuckers in our business? What have we been sniffing around in lately?"

"Whatever the fuck is going on around here might be more than we first thought. If they're making voice altering phone calls and shit like this is a damn action movie, we must be getting too close. But this crosses the fucking line, what does he mean what the commander was up to?"

Tyler was my wild child. He and the Commander had shared a close relationship, we all did, but Ty is everybody's problem child and we tend to keep them closer than most. If these fucks tried to blemish the Commander's name in anyway I'm pretty sure I'll have a hard as fuck time keeping him from going rogue.

"The money, it's got to be about the money we moved." It was a fuck load of money that we'd found in an account Dani's ex Robert and that Rosalind woman had set up using Dani's name. Quinn was still monitoring that shit to see what popped off, but so far nothing. We all knew that with that kind of money involved it wasn't gonna go down that easy, but it was a risk we'd had to take to smoke the fuckers out. I just thought we had more time, damn. Connor looked back towards his place where Dani was just coming out the door. She looked over and waved with a bright smile, then my door opened and Gaby came prancing out.

"Handle that Con. The rest of you know what to do. Gabriella, come here." She glanced over at me in surprise, probably because of the tone of my voice. The others scattered around the perimeter as she walked towards me. "I need you to stay inside today."

"But…" I just lifted my brow and that shut her up.
"Yes sir." I tapped her ass lightly to let her know I was pleased with her response, before pulling her in to kiss her forehead. "Good girl." We looked over to where I was sure Connor was telling his woman the same thing.

The women headed into Con's place while the brothers met in a huddle in the middle of the compound. "Change of plans, let's make sure this place is secure." I passed my phone off to Quinn. "Check this out, find out how this hump got my number and where that call came from."

Most people don't understand the strength of the technology the armed forces deal with. They see us as civilians without any backing now that we were stateside, but the reality was that my guys and I were always smart.

We brought shit home with us that we knew would come in handy when it came to protecting our asses as well as our families. Some of us had shit in our head that it would take a stick of dynamite to remove.

Each man went about his business making sure our shit was on lock. I called one of the men on the job to let them know we were either going to be late, or not there at all today, and to send someone else out to make the runs. The last job was almost done and we had a few more lined up after this, and were even at the point of turning people away.

All in all things were going fine except for the shit that was going on down by the water. We were accomplishing a lot of what we had set out to do, making strides. I wasn't about to let anything fuck with our program.

My brothers and I had been through the bowels of hell together, they see me as their designated leader and I take that shit seriously. No one was gonna get through me to hurt my family, fuck that.

"Everything looks cool Lo, but I say we take this shit as an eminent threat. Whatever this is I think this was the first volley, which means they're gonna come at us with more unless we back down, and I'm guessing we're not about to that shit right." Zak was usually quiet, but he was always ready for a good tussle. It had been a while since we'd kicked any major ass, except for Con's little skirmish a few weeks ago. Somehow these people had figured out what we were up to, and since the leak hadn't come from any of us, I'm guessing it was the asshole ex, the sidepiece, or Crampton. And since Crampton was bitch made, I'm more inclined to believe it was one of the other two.

"Con we have to go hunting, let's see if your boy was dumb enough to talk. Who do we have in NOLA that can nab the ratchet broad he was messing with?"

There was a lot of throat clearing which told me that I may or may not like what was coming next. The seven of us were a unit, but we dealt with other brothers in arms, sometimes people from other branches. Some of them were more fucked up than others, and we tend to attract the rougher element.

When all eyes turned to Zak I pretty much knew what was coming and so did he, from the reaction we got. "Fuck no, uh-uh anybody else, fuck, I'll go get the skel myself." Damn, I thought he was over this shit.

"Bro, we gotta do what we gotta do, and we don't have time for you to make that run and head back here. Where is she hiding out?" I turned to

JORDAN SILVER | 4

Quinn because he would be the best
one to give me what I needed since he
was the one keeping tabs on Rosalind
or whatever the fuck she was going by
these days.

"French Quarter a little place off
Chartres St. The place is old and noisy
as fuck and it's right in the middle of
the hustle and bustle of the tourist
crowd. I guess she learned her lesson
last time; but there's one thing she
missed, there's a balcony." He grinned
at that because Vanessa, the Lieutenant
we were planning to send after her,
wasn't called Cat-woman for nothing;
that chick could climb.

"Tell me you're okay with this
brother. We won't do it if you ain't but
we need her. Is she stateside Con?" He
looked at Zak as he nodded his head
and rocked back on his heels with his
hands stuffed in his pockets. "Man up
bro, stop being afraid of one little
woman, what is she four-eleven?" I
turned to scowl at everyone's pain in
the ass.

"Ty shut the fuck up, who said anything about being afraid?" Zak looked angry enough to chew nails. We all knew the story about Zak and Nessa, well some of it anyway. That was one tale he hadn't shared in its entirety. But we all knew that something had gone down between those two and whatever it was it had ended badly.

The way he was glowering at Ty he wasn't over shit, and knowing Nessa, she wasn't gonna back down either. I need this fuckery on top of everything else. But you gotta do what you gotta do. "Make the call Con. Zak, I expect you to be on your best behavior." It was short fucking notice but it looked like we were in the middle of some shit, now was not the time for bullshit. Fucking women.

"I'm cool, just keep her little ass in check when she gets here or I'm gonna finish what I started." He walked away after that cryptic note and I was already second-guessing my decision to bring her here.

If I knew more about what had gone down with them I could maybe try to mediate, but I didn't know shit. The only thing I was sure of is that another man wasn't involved, because had it been anything like that, my brother would've been court martialed already, so hopefully whatever it was wasn't too bad.

"Have any of you ever figured out what the fuck went down between those two?" I watched him storm towards the gym we all used. That more than anything told me what kind of mood he was in. Poor sap, she still had him tied up in knots.
"What always goes down between a male and a female Cap? I don't know the particulars but from what I remember about last time, this shit ought to be good. I'ma stock up on beer and popcorn, that shit was better than the movies, or more like ringside at a Heavyweight bout."

"Ty, anyone ever tell you you're a pain in the ass?"

"Nope, what I ain't is whipped like the rest of you fucks; looks like Zak's gonna be next. Y'all keep that wedding shit away from me ya hear, shit's catching."

Like I said, problem child. He loped of somewhere to give the rest of us peace of mind for a minute. He was joking and acting like everything was cool, but all of us knew to keep an eye on his high-strung ass. He was already wound tight about the Desert Fox business, and this would just be one more thing to bring out that fucker's crazy.

Chapter 4

LOGAN

We sat around in my kitchen all day working out strategy. It might've seemed like a bit much to anyone looking in from the outside, but we knew that every little thing meant something.

You learn that shit fast when you were in the thick of battle, returning enemy fire and your heart went out to the kid you saw trapped in the middle of the crossfires, only to see that same kid detonate when one of your fellow soldiers go to help. A couple episodes of that shit and you learn to be overly cautious about every damn thing.

Outwardly I was cool I had to be. I'd learned a long time ago that the boys followed my lead. It wasn't something that we were conscious of, but it was the truth nonetheless. If I was in a shit mood, they'd pick up on it, and that could sway the day for everybody. So if I let on that I was more upset by the caller's innuendo, then for sure they would be too. So I had to keep that shit close to the vest until I knew what was going on. Then I was gonna fuck somebody's shit up for trying to mar a good man's name.

A man who had done more for his country than most; especially some drug trafficking asshole.

"Okay so this is the first we're hearing about the Commander being involved in anything shady. First things first, we consider the source." I wrote that shit in big block letters on the power point board I had set up.

"Next, we know the Commander, he was basically in charge of whether we lived or died for a huge fucking chunk of our time when we were in, and he never let us down.

Aside from that, we knew the man, stand up as they come."

We were all in agreement that whatever this was-was nothing but a smokescreen. I wasn't sure what the locals knew or thought about what we did in the navy. It's a safe bet that the Commander never discussed missions and shit on the outside, but they had to at least know that you had to have nerves of steel to make it through fucking boot camp, farther more stay in for as long as the seven of us had.

"Devon I'm gonna need you to keep your ear to the ground, they seem to trust you around here more than they do the rest of us." That's because he had this deceiving, innocent boy next door look about him. With his nod I carried on.

"Until we know who said what and to whom, we can't really move, but we're not sitting around here on our asses waiting for them to make first strike. Con is right, it has to be about the money. We moved it, they start calling. That was a lot of fucking money; people commit horrendous acts for less so we know what we're up against.

From now on the women are under twenty-four hour guard. There will be no time when they are not under the eyes of one of us. They're always together anyway unless they're going off to work. Con make sure Dani takes a leave of absence or some shit, I'll work on Gaby. They can use the weddings as an excuse."

You'd think in the middle of this fuckery there would be no room for bullshit, but that didn't stop the five of them from making smart ass remarks about marriage.

"Moving right the fuck along, tonight we're gonna start with Robert, aka the douche." I don't know where we got a pic of this guy but we had one up on the board with a death arrow pointed at his head. I didn't have to think too hard to figure out whose handiwork that was. "I'm not sure he has the balls, but we're not taking any chances." They may think this shit was gonna have us running scared, and again, I don't know where they ever got the idea that we were pussies, but that phone call had the opposite affect to what they expected.

We threw around scenario after scenario but the reality was for now, all we could do was batten down the hatches and protect our flanks until we knew who the enemy was.

"You know what I'm thinking, I'm thinking somebody knows about our relationship with the commander. I'm not talking about the town's speculation as to why he left his team his land, but someone knows how any mark against him would affect us not only personally, but because of missions."

"Lo's right; the more I think about that call the more something stinks. We already know that this is no low-end operation they're too good. We can't even get a whiff of who these fucks are, and the people we've spoken to so far don't even seem to know who the fuck they're working for. I'm thinking that phone call was their first mistake, it gave us a little more insight than we had before."

"You're on to something there Con." I looked around at the rest of them, especially Ty who already looked like he was ready for battle, hotheaded little fuck. "Did you make that call?"

I kept my eye on Zak as I asked and almost rolled my eyes at his reaction. He was as prickly as a damn teenage girl on her period over this shit. "Yep, she's on it, said she was getting rusty since her retirement."

"Retirement? I didn't know about this." Vanessa was a little young to retire so that meant something serious had went down. I guess I'll have to wait until she showed up here to get the particulars. Zak seemed as stunned by the news as the rest of us, which meant he hadn't been keeping tabs on her. I wasn't even gonna go there with him right now, because that shit looked like it was gonna take a couple bottles of scotch at the very least.

"You know we never went through the Commander's stuff when we took over. It's still all locked away in the library of his place." Cord reminded me of something I hadn't thought of in a while.

None of us had wanted to go through the old man's personal papers and shit, felt too much like a violation of trust. So we'd locked everything away safely in his old home, which we had pretty much converted into an office with bedrooms and shit.

"What are you saying, that there's something there to verify this shit?" I sighed long and hard at Ty's outburst. This fucker is gonna give me agida. The only time he's actually calm and rational is when we're on a mission, any other time it's like dealing with a psych patient fresh off their meds; ADD fucker. "No Tyler that's not what he's saying. Look, we were all there; we all know the Commander was the salt of the earth. I think what your brother is saying is that maybe we've been coming at this thing all wrong.

None of us stopped to wonder if the old man was privy to any of this, if he suspected something or not. It's worth a look to see what if anything he knew. We just assumed that the old guys came to us first, but what if the Commander, who we know was highly intelligent, and extremely perceptive, was onto whatever this is?"

That seemed to calm his ass down and we were back on track. We decided that there was no point in putting that shit off once the decision had been made, so we sent Candy home early, which translated to her heading to Connor's house, where the women were gathered with their wedding shit.

***

GABRIELLA

"Okay Candy spill." I dragged her through the door after I'd spied her coming. I guess the guys had given her the day off because she was carrying her bag and the whole lot of them had descended on the old plantation house like the feds. "Lordy Gaby let me clear the door at least damn." Like I had time for that.

Dani and I have been on pins and needles ever since we were given our staying orders. It was gonna take me a while to get used to this mess, but with Logan there was no choice. Nothing I tried could sway that man from his path, he's as mule headed as one of my grandpa's old bulls.

I have wedding shit coming out my ears, first he curtailed how many hours I could spend running around, with his be home before dark dictate, and now he'd pretty much put me on house arrest. If I didn't love him like crazy already I'd brain him with something for even thinking he had the right.

"Don't nobody got time for that shit, what's going on over there?" Dani came in the living room with a tray of cookies and tea, like any decent southern belle would at a time like this.

Men are a slower breed, they do not understand the rigors of dealing with wedding plans and making sure that every little detail was just so.

Especially when you were planning a double wedding where two of the four participants just grunted and whined when asked for their input.

"Hey Candy, they got you too huh." Dani placed the tray down and sat with her prim and proper self like the lady of the manor. It amazes me that we had grown up together, been taught damn near the same things, and I had broken out of my shell and she hadn't. Don't get me wrong, Dani can get loose with hers if she has to, but she takes a little time to warm up. College had taken care of my good and proper thank you very much.

Being away from momma and daddy for the first time in my life, I'm not ashamed to say that I had gone buck-wild. The only thing I had kept was my virginity, because it had been drilled into me in my mama's milk that that belonged to the man I was gonna marry, everything else was up for dibs.

I drank, smoked, though I didn't like the taste of my first and only cigarette, went joyriding and everything else a delinquent teen with a bank account could get up to. It was some kind of cosmic joke I am sure that I had fallen and fallen hard for a man like my Logan. I couldn't fall for any of the milquetoast mamby-pamby saps in my circle, no I had to go and give my heart to Leonidas.

I had held onto my bad girl persona from my school days unlike Dani who was a born lady down her little pink toes. Logan likes to tease sometimes and ask how comes he'd ended up with the tomboy, but deep down I knew he needed someone like me to put up with his brand of crazy.

"I don't know what all's going on girls, you know these men, they're as tight lipped as they wanna be, but something's lit a fire under their asses. They ain't never had time for going through that place before, never showed much of an interest in it anyway, but now it seems they're hell bent for leather to get to 'em."

"Logan isn't talking and Dani says all Connor told her was not to leave the compound until farther notice. I sure wish I knew what was the big secret. You don't think it has anything to do with one of their missions do you?" I looked at Dani with a little fear in my eyes now. She reached out for my hand and squeezed.

"No, they would've told us if they were going away. I think this is about those night moves." She gave me a look, which I understood very well. Although he men trusted Candy, there were some things that were meant to be kept just between us, if they wanted her to know about their little secret rendezvous they'd let her in on it.

Logan had told me the bare minimum about that as well, and only because I needed to know where the hell he was leaving my bed to go to almost every damn night. It's not like he'd sat me down and talked me through it all nice like either no; if I remember correctly that conversation had gone something like, 'the boys and I have some shit to take care of and might have to leave at night for a while, I won't be gone long, there's nothing for you to worry about.' That was about it.

Candy didn't even ask any questions because she knew better and as much as I was dying to know, the talk soon turned to weddings. But while my two companions were discussing seating arrangements my mind was on what the men were up to. If Logan knew he'd have my ass, but I could never give up a good mystery.

All I needed was to get my girl Dani on my side and between the two of us we might be able to help. How bad can it be? This is Briarwood after all, nothing remotely interesting ever happens here.

Chapter 5

LOGAN

We spent a good part of the day going through the old man's shit and had yet to make a dent in it. Mostly we'd found old letters between him and his childhood sweethearts, and some from colleagues and shit like that, but there was nothing to raise any eyebrows so far. We worked through lunch or tried to, but the women descended upon us and browbeat us into taking a break.

I could tell my nosy ass princess was trying to sniff out what we were doing, but her sneak was as obvious as the nose on her face. Poor baby, it must be hell being surrounded by SEALs when you're accustomed to hoodwinking lesser men with a smile. That shit wasn't about to work, well except maybe with Ty, and since she was still shy about cooking, and the way to his heart was food, we were safe for now.

"Did you get anything done this morning baby?" She was sitting on my lap, swinging her feet as we ate our sandwiches that the girls had whipped up and drank lemonade mixed with iced tea. She looked about twelve with her hair in a ponytail and not a smidge of make-up on. I like seeing her like this, without the damn war paint that got onto everything.

"Nope, nothing at all. How long's this little hitch in my giddy-up supposed to last anyway?" I squeezed her around the middle, because although she said that shit all light, there was a hint of complaint in her voice.

"As long as I say." I waited for it because I know her, she can't leave shit alone for too long, I keep telling her one of these days that shit's gonna land her ass in trouble, but she's still convinced herself that she can get me to see things her way.

The others couldn't hear what we were saying thank fuck, because I would hate to have to deal with their shit if she gave me hell. "Logan we're trying to plan a wedding here. There are things that we need to be on site for, we can't just sit on our asses and expect them to get done. I understand your not wanting to participate, but now you're interfering with what I have to do and that's not fair."

I had to let that shit sink in to make sure she wasn't playing with me, or hadn't lost her damn mind, but she was dead ass serious. A look wasn't gonna cut it this time, but now wasn't the time either.

"We'll talk about this later." I tried to head shit off, the fuck I know about arguing with a female? In my mind, as her man, I lay down the rules, she follows, end of story. "What's there to discuss? I can give up today but…"

What the fuck? "I said later Gabriella." My tone had her deflating which usually would make me try to placate her, but this shit was serious, besides if I start letting her talk me into shit we'd both be in trouble. She wasn't too pleased when they left so we could get back to what we were doing.

"What's the matter Cap, your woman giving you fits?" I threw a piece of bread at Quinn and tried to escape. These fucks like to snick their noses in every damn thing, and the fact that she and I were whispering while the others were carrying on a conversation, would only get their antennas going. "Mind your own damn business you fuck."

"See what I told you, bitch made, both of them." Ty had to duck after making that statement because both

Con and I went after his ass. "Say Cap, you do know you're supposed to be the one in the tux right, you too Con." He thought his ass was funny. I cannot wait for him to fall. "As a matter of fact, I do, but I'm thinking of having my attendants, that would be you fucks, wear kilts on account of my Scottish blood."

"The fuck outta here with that shit Cap, I'm not wearing a skirt no matter what the fuck it's called." I knew that would shut him up. I also knew we were all trying to blow off steam before going back in. "Okay guys back to it."

There wasn't any of the usual banter between us; we were all pretty solemn once we passed the door into the private library that we had kept under lock and key since the night we'd buried our old friend.

This is the reason we had been putting this off, it was like saying the final goodbye, something that as tough as we all are, I didn't think we were quite ready to do. For the next few hours there was just more of the same, but then coming on to later in the evening, shit started to take a turn.

"Why the fuck was he writing in code? And check the dates, this was a little before he died, like a few months." Devon passed the ledger type book over to me and the rest gathered around to read over my shoulder.

Something that had been kept between the eight of us was a secret code. We'd all worked on it together and came up with basically our own language. It had been some time since any of us had used it, but it wasn't hard to decipher.

"Shit he suspected something." I ruffled through the pages getting little snippets here and there but I knew we were gonna have to go through it with a fine toothcomb.

"He knew we'd find this eventually, or have reason to come looking, that's why it's in our code. Whoever he suspected is very powerful for him to go to these lengths. Ty make copies for each of us will you?" I passed the book off to him and went back to my digging.

We were all more awake now that we knew we were on the right track. Poor commander, I wonder why he never said anything. We all spoke to him at least once a week when he was alive, even when we were on active we never lost touch, he was our father.

"Did he say anything to any of you about this?" They all shook their heads, which was pretty much what I expected. Our bond was such that there had never been any secrets between the eight of us.

We were each aware of our rank yes, but in the heat of battle, a bullet could give a fuck, so we'd learned to trust in each other beyond the titles. That meant that whatever the old man shared with me stateside, he would've shared with my brothers and vice versa.

***

We found a few more things that looked like they may be of interest, but then we broke away for dinner because the girls were getting grumpy. They knew some shit was going on but had no idea what.

I, as well as Connor was operating under the fact that they were on a need to know basis when it comes to this shit. They on the other hand like typical fucking females wanted to know everything, so they were playing the role since they didn't get their way. I guess after their little fishing expedition didn't turn up anything at lunch they had decided to change up the act. It was pissing me the fuck off.

I know just how to deal with Gabriella and her bullshit, what Con does with his woman is up to him. She tried coming out of her damn face in front of Quinn and Zak, asking my shit that I had already told her was none of her damn business.

"Are you trying to get fucked up?" She gave me the cold treatment after that. I saw Con whispering to his woman and she was nodding like she had some damn sense. How the fuck did I end up with the hardheaded one?

"Damn, it's like the arctic in this bitch, what did you two do now?" Cord slapped Ty on the back of the head for being stupid and saved me the trouble. The idiot didn't realize yet that when the women get like this it was best to ignore their shit until they came to their damn senses, either on their own, or with a little help. He'll learn, just as soon as he finds one that ties his ass in knots and he learns the difference between a jump off and a wife.

"Taste good ladies, you outdid yourselves." I guess Con decided to play the diplomat, then again that shit might work with Dani, she's easy going and pays heed to her man when he says some shit to her. Gaby on the other hand thinks she can stand toe to toe with me.

Poor thing, I've been letting her get used to me, giving her time to settle in. There was no point in scaring the shit out of her before I even got the damn ring on her finger.

But I was afraid before the night was over she was gonna see another side of me. Especially since she was letting her displeasure show in front of others, that's a big fucking no-no.

By the end of the night when the boys had left and the place was secure, my mind was winding down a bit. And by that it I mean I had more time to think about what the fuck that hump was up to and gave my anger free reign. I sometimes have to hold my shit in check, when you're looked up to as a leader, especially with strong men, you can't always show your hand.

I know in certain situations they feed off of me, and where I'm going in my head, so I have to keep it on the low. But now that they were gone, I didn't have to hold back any longer, I could let my shit out and I knew just how to release the stress.

"You, come 'ere." She didn't know what hit her. She'd been puttering around the kitchen cleaning shit that didn't need cleaning, which told me she had a suspicion that her ass was in trouble.

But whether she knew why she was getting what was coming or not didn't mean fuck all to me. I nabbed her around her neck and pulled her into me for the first mouth fuck. I sent my tongue damn near to the back of her throat before releasing her. "In the bedroom, now." She knew what that shit meant and she wasn't looking too sure of herself as she headed off in that direction.

I started stripping in the hallway and it was safe to say my dick didn't need any direction; he was already on the prowl, sticking out in front of me with a pearl of pre-cum already forming at his tip. She was down to her skimpy panties when I cleared the doorway.

"Leave them." I was in that kind of mood, and I didn't forget that there was supposed to be a lesson in there for her somewhere. Somebody might not get their jollies tonight, I wasn't sure yet. I do know she hates me to leave her high and dry; my baby is a climax freak. If she could cream all over my dick twenty-four seven she would, but a fucker's gotta eat and other shit.

I walked over to her, still holding a little of myself back. I couldn't unleash on her after all, that would be fucked up. But she was gonna get some of it. If she hadn't acted up all damn evening I might've given her a severe dicking, which meant she would've walked twisted for a day at most, but with her bad behavior and my fucked up mood, she was looking at a pussy pounding, and a pussy pounding is nothing to sneeze at.

First things first though! "Kneel." She looked up at me as she got to her knees in front of me. "You know what to do." She knew from my tone that she wasn't allowed to touch me with anything but her mouth. Her hands went behind her back and her head bobbed forward, mouth open wide to take me in. She sucked on my cockhead first, getting her cream, then pulled back and licked from tip to base and back. She nibbled on my dick being careful not to nip me with her teeth too hard before swallowing my shit in one gulp.

My hands went to her hair and fisted and I started face fucking her hard. She made gulping sounds as she tried to keep up as drool and pre-cum leaked all over her face; that was one of my favorite looks.

"Hold it." I was at the entrance to her throat when I stopped her, and then I slowly eased in all the way. There was an art to this shit unless you wanted to hurt your woman; I wasn't into that shit.

A pussy can take more of a beating than a throat I think. What I did do, was flex my cock in her neck until she balked and choked, but with my hands in her head keeping her in place she had no choice but to deal. Lesson one.

I pulled out of her neck and looked down at her sternly as she looked up at me a little more weary now that she sensed my mood. I tapped her cheek with my twelve and a half inch rod and ran the tip over her lips, leaving pre-cum to dry there. "Up on your hands and knees." She climbed onto the bed and looked over her shoulder.

"The fuck you looking for? Eyes front." I knew this way the anticipation would kill her, she didn't know what I was about to do back there.

I eased in behind her and grabbed her ass cheeks and spread. I saw her tense because she knows I said I won't take her there since the one time we tried she was in pain for hours and I had barely got my tip in.

I played with her cheeks long enough to get her worried, and then took my cock in hand and rubbed it up and down her drooling slit. I like the way her hips and thighs jerk a little when I do that, so I did it again. I teased her with my cock tip, using my fingers under her belly to play with her clit while I eased just the tip into her pussy before pulling back.

I kept that shit up for a good five minutes until she started to relax, then I slammed into her forcefully. I had to hold onto her so she didn't slide across to the other side of the mattress from the force of my thrust.

Now she looked back wide eyed like 'what the fuck?' I used the opportunity to wrap her long mane around my fist and pull on her hair hard enough to sting, while going into her belly with the next stroke. Oh she was scared now. "Logan…"

"Shut up." She whimpered and tried spreading her legs wider to ease some of the pressure but a hard slap on her ass soon had her changing her mind. "Stay where the fuck I put you. I want you to think about what the fuck you did wrong while I fuck the shit out of you." The shit probably wasn't gonna work because her pussy was already doing overtime in the leaking department. She was tight as fuck too around my dick, choking me off in her fear.

"Relax your pussy muscles or it's gonna go bad for you." I slapped her ass again when she didn't obey me fast enough.

"I can't, please I'm sorry." I'm sure she was but it was too late for an apology, she shouldn't have started her shit in the first damn place. I used my fingertips on her swollen clit to soften her up a bit.

I nibbled my way around her ear and down her neck, leaving my mark there, all the while plotting to loosen her up so I could put a hurting on her pussy that she won't soon forget.

As soon as I felt the give in her, that slight easing of her flesh, I made my way in there nice and easy; just another one of my tactics to get her to let her guard down.

I turned her head so I could feed her my tongue and slid it past her lips. She sucked as her pussy opened up even more and that's when I struck. I swallowed her screams of disbelief as I let my dick do the talking.

A heavy dick at full hardness can be a serious weapon in times like these, and though she'd gotten her ass in trouble before, it was nothing like this shit.

The secret to this shit wasn't just the pounding either. When your woman was accustomed to being taken care of, was used to loving touches no matter how rough the sex was, you take that shit away she notices. There were no whispered words of praise, no soft smiles, and my touch was as impersonal as it was possible to get. I held even my grunts and moans in check; in short I gave her nothing; just the steel length of my cock butting against her cervix.

When I felt my nuts beginning to draw up, I pulled out of her quickly for my crowning glory. I sprayed the small of her back, tapped the last dregs off on her ass cheek and hopped off the bed headed for the shower.

Her tears started before I left the room. That'll teach her disrespectful ass to show out in front of our family or anyone else for that matter.

Especially since everything I did was to protect and keep her safe. If I gave even an inch with this one I'd spend most of my day getting her out of shit; she's one of those.

She must've hit one of the other bathrooms because when I came back she was in bed, all fresh and sweet smelling. I didn't say shit to her as I got dressed in the dark for what I had to do. I felt her eyes on me but was still too pissed to care. I wasn't only mad at her, but at the situation. This was the very reason why all of us had promised never to settle down while we were in.

I thought we were out of that shit now, but it seemed trouble had followed us here as well.

There was no way for me to get her to understand my side of things, how could she? Most women were accustomed to their man opening up about shit at the dinner table, discussing their day and their business like regular people, we weren't gonna have that, not when it came to shit like this.

I left the room and the house, making sure to secure her inside until I got back. We were moving under cover of dark so no one would know we were off the compound since we were using a secret exit route. I still wasn't too happy about leaving the women here unguarded so we left Cord on night watch. He didn't even grumble about missing the action because he knew how important this was to me and Con.

Robert the fuck had disappeared off the grid for a minute but we found him again. The idiot was so unoriginal that he'd moved to a town over on the other side from the one he'd use to live in before. It was just as easy breaking into his place this time as it had been the last, I guess unlike his partner in crime, he hadn't really learnt that lesson well.

"Hello asshole." Connor waited until he was standing over him in the dark with a penlight pointed at him. He came awake with a start and you could almost smell the fear coming off of him. He sat up like someone had prodded his ass and almost broke the damn headboard. He wasn't looking too good either I noticed, looked like someone had fisted his face. "Who worked you over Robert?" I figured I should try to get at least that much out of him before Con pulverized his ass just for being.

"Not you again, what do you guys want, haven't you caused enough trouble?"
"Are you really that fucking stupid? We weren't the ones who got in bed with these assholes that was all you. You're lucky you're still breathing after what you tried to do to my woman, now who the fuck worked you over asshole?"

"I told you before I don't know. You think you're working for one guy, but then he's working for another guy and another and another. I don't know who is who I swear, just please just leave me alone I'm sorry I ever got involved." He wiped his hand under his nose and my stomach turned, what an absolute sap.

"Why did you?"
"Why did I what?" Damn, he's so stupid I almost felt sorry for him. He turned his frightened eyes my way, I

guess he figured anything was better than Con. "Why did you get involved?" We hadn't really got much out of him the last time, but then we hadn't yet realized how big this thing really was. Back then we were more focused on the money laundering thing and why Dani's name was being used.

"It was fast money."
"How did they approach you?" I kept my voice civil unlike some people who were looking at him like he was a specimen they'd like to extinguish. "I told you already the last time."

"Tell me again." I got closer to the bed so he could see what there was of me to see. We were all painted up pretty good and covered in black from head to toe. I guess it was our approach that had given us away.

"Someone contacted me, I guess they knew about me and Dani…"
"Don't say her fucking name."

"Con…" I gave him a look, which I'm sure he missed in the dark, but he got the message, stand the fuck down. I expected him to pound this douche into dust any second but I was hoping to get more out of him first.

"Uh…" he looked at Con like he was a two headed monster and moved closer to my side. "Okay um, they knew about the charity and that I might have a way in.

They said she wouldn't get hurt I swear." Again he looked at his own personal monster before carrying on with the story. "We were only supposed to move some numbers around, no one would've ever known if you guys hadn't gone snooping. That last time wasn't the first time we'd done it, we'd made a few dry runs before to see how things would pan out."

"Get to what we wanna know before this one takes your head off." Con was looking like he was ready to go all Samurai on his ass, and I wasn't sure I wouldn't let him. This guy was a real piece a work. "Like I said, someone contacted me."

"How, by mail, email, over the phone how?"
"Oh, they called the first time."
"And why did you take the offer?" He got the beady eye syndrome then. You know, when the eyes get smaller and start flitting around like prey looking for a predator.

"I was in a tight spot okay, I needed the money."
"Who knew you needed money?"
"My bookie I guess, why? You can't be thinking it's Clancy, that fool wouldn't know how to run a set up like this, I'm telling you, these guys are professionals."

I was inclined to believe the idiot and the more we pushed him the more convinced I was that he was telling the truth. He was just another hump who'd fallen in with the wrong crowd. For me, I'd just leave his dumb ass alone and be done with it, but Con had an axe to grind. "Let's go sailor." He gave the douche one last glower before following me out the room.

"Why won't you let me end him?"
"Because it's not right?"
"The fuck you care?" I tried not to laugh because I knew what his problem was, it was eating him up that Dani had once been with this guy, but I can't have my men going around killing off exes, how many virgins were they expecting in this bitch anyway? That brought my mind back to my own pain in the ass.

"Women are a pain in the fucking ass." I signaled to the others to fall in from their positions in the dark outside the townhouse as I made my way to the truck. "Okay I'll bite why do you say that? Gaby giving you fits?" I could hear the laughter in his voice, disrespectful fuck. "When isn't she giving me fits? What the hell is wrong with them, well not yours, Dani's a saint, I ended up with the menace." He stopped short and looked at me with his mouth open before breaking out in laughter.

"What the hell's so funny? She is." The others wanted to know what the joke was so I filled them in while Con tried to compose himself. Of course I had to listen to all of Gabriella's virtues and how a beast like me should be glad she'd even spit in my direction.

"Fuck you Ty, you're just hanging on for those cheese biscuit things Dani says she makes." Which I have yet to taste myself, because she's got problems, fucking nut.

"And, your point? All I'm saying is that both little sisters could've done a lot better." Con and I had to listen all the way home in the truck with the rest of those idiots to how lacking we were, and how much better off our women would've been if they'd chosen one of them. The mood was so light it didn't even matter than we hadn't learned anything more than we'd already known. Well except that we were right in our thinking that this wasn't a small operation.

That led me to thinking about what else they could be in to. If we followed the waterway to the neighboring towns will we find more of the same? How did they come to choose this place anyway? Was it a local? That possibility was looking more and more real.

"We're idiots; of course it's someone local, or at least one of them is. How else would they have known about Dani's charity and now the call about the Commander? Not to mention Robert the douche said they knew about his little gambling problem."

That changed the subject again and we put our heads together trying to figure out who had that kind of pull in the small town. Both Con and I were dating the daughters of two of the town's leading families, but I didn't see them for this, and Con had already vetted his in-laws when that whole thing had gone down.

We were looking for someone else and I was pretty sure it wasn't Gaby's dad, but I was still gonna look to be absolutely certain.

We hadn't gone that deep into the ledger we'd found or the other papers as yet. So far all we had was that the old man had suspected something was going on down by the water. There were a lot of dates and numbers that we were gonna have to figure out at some point, but no smoking gun pointing to any one person in particular.

The commander also wasn't a foolish man, so if he was onto something he might've left us the ledger with our secret code, but there's a good possibility there were other writings somewhere else, more well hidden. The fucking place was huge I wouldn't even know where to start, but maybe there was something in the book.

"I think we have to get to the bottom of that ledger and soon. The sooner we translate that shit, the closer we will be to the truth. If the old man suspected something then this thing might've been going on for a while. We need to find out what he saw, what made him suspicious, because we all know he wouldn't let something like this rest."

"I'm with you there Lo, looks like we got two breaks in one day, first the phone call, tipping us off to the fact that we're getting too close and now the ledger." Connor sped through the night headed for home and our women and who knows what the fuck else. I was getting really tired of the bullshit. In the service you pinpoint the enemy and take that fucker out. I didn't have time for this bullshit.

Chapter 6

LOGAN

It was full dark when we pulled in. Cord said all had been quiet and there was nothing to report. We made one last round around the perimeter before calling it a night. I slipped into the house quietly so as not to awaken her, and got undressed in the dark. Out of habit, I made the rounds around my place as well before heading for m woman and bed.

I got in on my side and since I was still a little pissed at her, didn't pull her into my arms the way I usually do. I guess I wasn't quiet enough because she stirred behind me. "Logan?" She snuck up to my back and did her kitten shit where she's all cute and cuddly. Sneaky ass.

"What is it?" my voice was stern and uninviting because if she made the

wrong move, or the right one
depending on how you look at it, I'd
be putty in her damn hands and
tonight's little lesson would be in vain.
"I'm sorry I was bad I won't do it
again."
"Yes the fuck you will. Go to sleep."
I'll forgive her in the morning. Right
now I had a misbehaving woman to
train.

***

I rolled over early the next day
before the sun rose. She was still
sound asleep with tear tracks on her
face. Poor baby, she must think I'm
really mad at her. I don't remember
ever not holding her all night since we
started sharing a bed. She was so
beautiful in the early morning light
that filtered through the windows, and
so fucking young. She certainly didn't
look like she was able to take on a man

like me, but she did it very well. My badass baby.

I made my way under the sheet that she had around her hips. Damn she has the prettiest skin, soft and supple with a hint of honey from the summer sun. I kissed her hip once before easing her onto her back. She sighed and settled as I held my breath.

Don't wake up, not yet. I checked to make sure she was still asleep. I wanted to take my time and enjoy this, but if her greedy ass were awake she'd rush me to get to the dick.

"Damn baby what the fuck?" Her pussy was a red puffy mess. It looked like I'd literally pounded her with my shit. I studied her for a minute to make sure she wasn't torn or some shit, and tested her skin with the tip of my finger for heat. I'm gonna have to make this shit up to her. That's what happens when I turn off in the middle of a punishment, I can go too far. Damn Logan you fuck. The one person you're supposed to have control with you lose it.

I ran my nose along her flesh and inhaled her scent. My morning wood got even harder at the sight and smell of her. I opened her with my fingers and inspected the damage. I must've been really ice last night because I didn't realize I was hitting it that hard.

I looked down at my cock trying to do a Jedi mind trick on his ass to see if he would behave, but that shit wasn't even close to working. He'd already smelt his girl and there was no putting him back in the gate. I'm gonna have to give her the softest fuck in creation, or she'd walk bow legged for a week.

I licked her folds before opening her slit and letting my tongue go inside. I was careful not to be too rough as I let the flat of my tongue taste her morning dew. She made

JORDAN SILVER | 9
7

waking noises when I took her ass in my hands and lifted her to my mouth. By the time she came fully awake I had my tongue buried to the hilt and my fingers digging into her ass.

I took care of her the best I could, tonguing her pussy's soreness away as I pressed my cock into the mattress for some relief. She wasn't fully awake yet, but there was a smile on her face. She knew if her man was giving her an early morning tongue bath that he couldn't be that mad any more. I'm such a damn sap.

She moved against my tongue, slowly at first, and then the pleasure hit her and she went wild. I like the wanton moves she makes when she can't control herself. The way she spreads her legs wider without having to be told, the way her nails dig into my scalp as she tries to keep me just where she needs me. I especially like the way she moves, like she's fucking herself on my tongue.

I pressed my cock into the bed because she wasn't ready to take me yet, not by a long shot. So I tried to keep my dog on its leash while I pleasured her with my tongue until I had taken some of the sting from the night before out of her abused pink pussy; well it was more like red now but…

"Can you take me now?" My mouth and jaw was tired as fuck and I know her greedy ass would keep me down there with my face buried in her snatch all day, it wouldn't be the first time, but I had shit to do. Her answer was to tug on my shoulders to pull me up her body. One last check showed that she wasn't as beaten up looking as she was when I started, but she was still a little swollen

I eased my cockhead in slowly, sort of testing the waters so to speak. She was a tight fucking fit, tighter than usual. "Baby, if this hurts you gotta tell me and I'll stop."

Her lying ass nodded but I knew she was full of shit. I measured her pain and discomfort by watching her eyes myself. That's how I knew to stop when there was only about six inches, half my dick, inside her; anything more and she started flinching.

"Wait a minute love." I pulled out and reached for the side drawer. I rummaged around until I found the cock ring I was searching for and slipped it on to the desired length. I eased back inside her with more confidence, this way I was sure not to hurt her.

Sometimes I get carried away when the pussy's good, and the pussy's always good. I didn't want to forget and slam my whole length into her and hurt her unnecessarily, this way the ring would block me from going too far.

Unlike last night, this was a slow sweet ride. I held her close with her face in my neck with one hand on her ass keeping her close, and the other around her shoulders. You couldn't get a thin blade of grass between us that's how close we were.

"I missed you baby." I'm not a complete ass I know how to make my woman feel her worth. "I missed you too." She squeezed me a little tighter as I cautioned myself not to get too rough.

When I came, I brought her over the edge with me. We stayed locked together like that for a long time until the birds started chirping and I started moving inside her again. "You too sore for this?" She shook her head no and pushed her pussy harder onto my cock. "Quit it before your hurt yourself." I tried slowing her ass down. "I want all of you, please Logan, I can take it I promise." I studied her eyes and tested her with a harder stroke before pulling out and removing the ring.

I was still a gentleman when I dipped my dick back into her though, but she had other ideas. Her nails bit into my ass, she planted her feet in the mattress and her pussy took over. "Gabriella, fuck."

For five minutes she fucked herself on my dick, I didn't move, didn't do a damn thing but hung over her as she got what she needed out of me. She laughed like a loon when she came. I like when she does that shit. "You done?" I slammed into her, cutting her off mid laugh. "Oh shit." Yeah!

I pulled her nails out my ass and held her hands down on the bed over her head. "Wrap your legs around my back." She hurried to obey and as soon as she did I started fucking. I was riding high in her pussy, hitting the back of it with each stroke, making her cream the way she does. She begged me to fuck her harder, but I kept it to a decent pace so as not to hurt her again. "Shh baby it's okay." She was reaching for her climax and close to tears because I wasn't going faster to help her out.

She growled some shit at me that got her a slap on the ass before I flipped us over. "Go ahead greedy, take what you need." Her eyes lit up and she bit into that bottom lip of hers which meant I was in for it now.

That's her 'I'm about to be a bad girl' look. She started out slow, lifting herself on and off my pole, then rocking herself back and forth, looking for her sweet spot with my dick. When she found it, it was off to the races. Still I held her hips to control her wild movements, but I didn't try to stop her.

"Uhhh, harder Logan, faster." Her head went back on her neck, her tits pushed forward, and beads of sweat were starting to form on her skin. I wasn't thinking when I sat up suddenly to reach her tits with my mouth, but that seemed to be the right move.

It sent my dick deeper into her, hitting her spot even as I sucked her nipple into my mouth hard. She gushed all over my dick, riding hell bent for leather. "Oh it's so good, feels so good." She did her babbling shit while I fucked up into her, chasing my own cum.

I felt it rise up in me, hot and sweet and blasted her insides. It was like a tidal wave this morning, a never ending fountain of jizz spewed up inside her while I pulled her down hard onto my rod until my nuts were empty. She kept moving to get the most out of my still hard cock until she damn near exhausted herself. "Hop off." I tapped her ass to get her moving. "You need a shave let's go."

She lifted off my dick and plopped down on her back beside me. "I'll just lie here, you do it." I kissed her forehead before rolling out of bed and heading bare-assed for the bathroom.

"Two minutes, be in here." She mumbled something and rolled over onto my pillow, burying her face in my scent. I watched her for a hot minute, enjoying the feeling in my heart. Never in a million years, not even after seeing Connor get taken down, did I ever think this shit was in the works for me. Now I can't imagine life without her in it.

Isn't it strange how that shit works? How you can go from accepting and believing one thing about yourself to knowing something else entirely? When she wasn't tying me in knots, she was making me crazy. It seemed like twenty of the twenty-four hours I was given in a day were now consumed with thoughts of her. Everything was about her, what she needed, how to keep her safe, and a whole host of other shit that I never thought to be dealing with ever in this lifetime.

I'd seriously thought that my brothers and I would settle down peacefully in this little slice of heaven and live out our days away from the chaos and mayhem we'd endured while in the service. I don't think any of us ever expected to settle down and have families though we talked about it back in the day.

We had too much shit going on, had seen too much of the worse of what mankind had to offer. Now I'm looking forward to planting my kid inside her. The shit doesn't even break me out in a cold sweat anymore.

She pranced into the bathroom with my seed drying on her inner thigh, and her hair flowing wildly around her shoulders. "Let me clean you up first." Who would've thought that one of the highlights of my day would be washing her body? For some reason I get a huge thrill out of grooming her. She stood still while I washed between her legs getting her nice and clean for her shave.

Of course as soon as she was clean and sweet smelling, I knelt at her feet and with the water running down on my head and back, lifted her leg over my shoulder and tongue fucked her again. I'd only planned to get her off one last time before we started our day, she didn't need to be riding my dick anymore for the day, but she started making those fuck me noises and tugging at me to come get some.

I stood and slid in in one smooth motion. Pinning her against the cool wall, I kept one of her legs over the crook of my arm and left the other on the floor, while I fucked her with my whole dick and sucked hard on her nipple. "Oh fuck oh fuck oh fuck." Have you ever seen a good girl gone bad? That shit is a big fucking turn on, turning little Ms. Priss into my own little cum addict.

With her tit in my mouth and my dick buried to the hilt in her pussy it didn't take her long to cum. As soon as she came down I released her tit and whispered in her ear. "I want to cum in your mouth." I pulled out and she dropped to her knees just in time to catch my first load on her tongue.

Then my little debutante covered just the head of my cock with her lips, held them closed tight and sucked, as I offloaded in her mouth. "Show me." She held her head back and opened her mouth before swallowing while holding my eyes with hers. "Naughty girl." I pulled her up finished cleaning her up and tried my best to stay the fuck away for her pussy. I had shit to do.

After I was through with her I took care of myself before stepping out and getting the supplies ready for her shave. Fuck, I'm gonna be late again. I looked down at my boy and he was remembering that swallow and looking for seconds, greedy fuck. Between my dick and her greedy ass pussy I'm headed for an early grave.

Chapter 7

LOGAN

"Devon and Cord, you two have first watch, we can't let the job go too many days without us being there, and we're not leaving the women here alone." Of course they nodded their agreement and the rest of us headed out. I missed her ass already and we hadn't even cleared the gate.

This was more about leaving her alone while all this shit was going on than anything else. We were gonna look through the ledger this evening after dinner, but we couldn't leave the job alone too many days in a row since it was coming on to the end and we make it a point not to do shoddy work. The only way to make sure of that shit was to handle things yourself.

Business wise we couldn't complain, things had taken off in ways that none of us had expected, not in the middle of a recession anyway, but so far so good.

We did good work and that spoke for itself, not to mention our reputation seemed to be spreading in the right circles and that shit goes a long way. My phone rang as we were on the road and I thought, 'not a fucking again.' But I recognized the number.

"Hey Lo, I just heard from Nessa. She's moving in tonight, should be here tomorrow, next day the latest." I whistled over the phone, I'd expected at least a couple days wait, but I should've known better.

One thing about Vanessa, she gets the job done. "Sounds good, how's our boy?" it's not like I expected Zak to do anything foolish, but when it came to men and women, I was beginning to see that that shit didn't follow any guidelines I'd ever encountered. Pretty much everything else on earth had a playbook except that.

"He seems cool, I didn't tell him yet though, I'll get on it as soon as we get to the site." We hung up and I paid attention to where we were going. We weren't expecting to be ambushed or anything like that, but we weren't taking any chances either. The hump hadn't called back and nothing else seems to have been done, but if they were on to us, we had to be on the alert.

At the site we looked over what had been done in our absence the day before and I was glad to see that the men and women we had working with us hadn't slacked while we weren't here. That was always a good look and meant we could promote men and women as needed.

Each man went to his own thing to get the job done. Nothing like hard, back breaking work, I'd take this shit over the jungles of the world any day, and I never thought I'd be saying that shit. In fact until a few weeks ago, before we got the call about the Desert Fox, I was kinda getting itchy about being out of the loop. Now that I had Gaby, I was looking at that shit different.

As I pounded nails my mind wandered between the shit that was going on and Gabriella. She was all focused on this wedding shit and I knew before it was all said and down, she was gonna have me like a little bitch, then Ty won't ever shut the fuck up about bitch made and all the other bullshit anecdotes he came up with.

I wanted to give her the wedding of her dreams, but when the fuck did that involve me getting all the way involved in that shit? I thought all I had to do was give her cash, show up on the day and say 'I do' and be out. Connor that fuck had been with me on this when the girls first talked about doubling up, now it looks like Dani had worked on his ass and if he fell then my woman was gonna get her tits in a twist if I didn't. I'd have to hear all about how I don't love her as much as Con love Dani and all that other female shit they use to make us stupid. Fucking female.

"Whose go is it?" it was lunchtime and I had pissed myself the fuck off with my own thoughts. I threw my gloves to the side and emptied a bottle of water with one swallow. "It's hot as a bitch in this fuck. The fuck are you fools looking at?"

"What's up with you Cap, somebody piss in your Wheaties or some shit?" Zak and his tongue twisting ass, when he does talk he gives my ass a headache. "The fuck are you talking about?"
"Your face bro, you mad about something?"
"No, it's Dani and this wedding bullshit." Why the fuck that should

make them laugh was beyond my ass, I think the sun was too hot or some shit.

"What does she want you to do? You not talking about that kilt fuckery again are you?" I gave Ty the stink eye for being an asshole. "No she wants me to help pick out flowers. Somebody agreed with me that we weren't getting involved in this shit, but now it looks like they're all in.' Connor the fuck didn't even have the decency to look ashamed.

"Told you about those bitch made fuckers you can't trust them." "Can somebody please keep his ass off the TV, he never learns anything good from that shit." I'd like to meet the fucker that taught Ty that bitch made shit so I could bitch slap their ass into next week.

"Look Lo, the way I see it, this wedding shit is only for one day. I say give the girls what they want this one time and get on with our lives."

"See, bitch made."

"Whatever asshole, all I'm saying is that when your woman looks at you all gooey eyed and say 'but baby why don't you care about our wedding?' You show her that you fucking care."

"You've lost your fucking mind, we do this shit they'll have us doing some pussy whipped shit next. Don't you get it? with you it's the eyes with me it's the fucking lip, just don't look in her eyes unless you wanna get trapped into doing some shit you don't want, that's how I deal with that one and her shit."

"I don't know Lo, it doesn't seem like such a big deal to me." I caught the look on his face just in time. "Fucker are you setting me up?" I looked at the rest of them as they started exchanging fist pounds. "I told them you'd never go for it. Fuck you I'm picking out flowers, Dani knows better than that shit the fuck."

Woo, thank fuck I was beginning to wonder about my brother. "So whose turn is it to get lunch, and we never discuss this wedding shit again."
"Con's."
"The fuck is it always my go, Ty you're up."
"Uh-uh brother, I had Monday, later for that shit." He was a little more annoyed than the situation warranted, which caused some raised brows.

"What's with you bro, you on the rag?" I have to keep an eye on this one for more reasons than one. Lately he's been getting agitated more easily. I thought it was because of the mission that's been hanging over our heads, but this didn't feel like it had anything to do with that.

Quinn's stupid ass grin told me I was missing something. "What?"
"He's afraid of the little hottie that works at the diner." I rolled my eyes when the fuckery started. It never ceased to amaze me how grown men

who'd served together in some of the most dangerous situations known to man could degenerate into high school pedantic assholes when it came to females.

"Fuck you I'm not afraid of anyone."
"Are you blushing Ty, what the fuck?"
"Give me the damn list Lo; asshole."
That last was thrown at Quinn along with a left hook, which he ducked. "Never a dull fucking moment, and on that note." I turned to Zak who looked like he was deep in thought about something. "Zak, Vanessa will be here sometime tomorrow or the day after, we cool?"

He didn't look too sure there for a second and I wondered again just what the fuck had gone down between those two. From what I could remember, the two of them had been hot and heavy there for a while, which had been surprising considering the deal we'd made with each other as a team. I guess it had been acceptable because Vanessa was one of us, maybe not the same branch, but we were fighting for the same cause.

Unlike a civilian female she would understand the rigors and the ins and outs of the life.

Then one day it was like world war fucking four and the only reason things hadn't escalated was because the shit went down while we were on a mission and both of them had to be mindful of their rank and where the fuck they were. After that, nothing! I don't think he even mentioned her name after that last day. As mush as I like Vanessa, if there were any other way to do this, I would've gone with it.

"I'm cool Lo don't start worrying about me I'm a big boy. Just let's get to the bottom of this shit once and for all. I feel like there's too much bullshit going on around us just lately, and we came here hoping to get away from that shit."

He composed himself very well but he wasn't fooling me. Hopefully whatever was going on between those two could be resolved this time. For now, I tabled it and focused on the issue at hand.

"I'm with you brother. The rest of you keep your eyes and ears open. Shit, I shoulda sent someone else with Ty." I wasn't thinking, didn't think that anyone would go after one of us, especially not in broad daylight, but still. "From now on we do everything in twos until we've resolved this shit."

Our talk with Robert last night only made me more uneasy. When there was that much secrecy involved and for so long, that left some serious implications. The only ones I know that could keep an operation like this under the radar for so long were governments and big time corporations.

Dealing with either is always a pain in the ass, and sometimes the only way to dismantle the shit was to cut off the snake's head, literally.

"You think the commander found anything? If he was on the case you know he'd never give up." We all had an opinion on that, and were pretty much in agreement.

The old man would never have left any stone unturned if he thought there was something illegal going on, especially in his little town. "He got sick though remember, so that could've brought his little PI game to an end. Whatever he found though it's a safe bet that we're gonna find it in the ledger or somewhere else in the house. I think it's time we went through the place, maybe give Candy a few days off with pay. Dev can handle the books for that long at least, can't you Dev?"

"Of course Cap, I say we table everything else and get to the bottom of this shit. The job here's almost done, not much more to it but the superficial stuff anyway and we have the right people for that." The guys all nodded their agreement and I guess that was that.

Ty came back with the grub and he didn't look any worse for wear so I guess the hot little number that's been giving him fits for a while hadn't done him any harm.

For someone with so much damn lip, that boy sure had a yellow streak a mile wide when it came to that one little girl. Now wasn't the time to rib him about it though, we had a lot to deal with. Of course the talk turned to our little night missions and the fact that we were still no closer to finding out what all was going on there, and none of us were going to rest easy until we did.

It was a pain in the ass to go around in circles when you were accustomed to taking care of shit in and orderly and timely fashion. "My only problem with the whole thing is not knowing shit. How can we let the women walk around freely when we don't know who the fuck is who? It could be someone they know and trust. If that is true, and we know these people are onto us, then their asses are in danger."

"Well we know it wasn't Robert the ass that snitched so I guess it was the woman. But with both of them claiming not to know who's pulling their strings where do we start to look?" I looked to Quinn after Ty's little speech since he was the one in charge of tracing the call. "So far that shit's bouncing off of a million different places. Whoever these people are they're good, we're not gonna get them that easily that's for sure. I can get to the source, but it's gonna take time. They have a shitload of interfaces blocking shit."

"So we're dealing with hi-tech shit is what you're saying, almost as good as ours."
"Basically, yeah." Shit, just what I was afraid of.
"Damn, that confirms my theory. This isn't a mom and pop operation, not some low-end dealer running shit.

Not that we thought it was, but it would've been nice if we caught a break. If the shit had been going on for as long as we believe, not to mention the way they set up Dani's family charity, that shit takes brains and skills.

Someone very powerful has a hand in this shit, and I'm afraid their next move is gonna be to use the Commander and his memory in some way not to our liking before all is said and done. If that should happen, I want everyone to keep their head. Ty, I'm gonna need you to go to your happy place." I got the finger for that one but I still gave his brothers the look over his head and received their nods of understanding.

Everyone knew to keep an eye on him, it was one thing to let him hotdog it in the hills of Kabul but the streets of Georgia were a whole other story. "We know the man, so nothing they say is gonna matter.

We know how this shit works we've done it ourselves more than once. It's all blowing smoke, a way to keep us focused on their bullshit while they do whatever the fuck it is they're trying to do here."

"Agreed, no one goes off base here. We all keep our heads and stay focused. No one does anything without all of us knowing about it; no one goes off on their own anywhere. For the next little while we're on lock. They might not be expecting us to take it that far, but that's what the fuck we're gonna do, we're gonna treat this like any other Op."

Connor had gone into command mode. I guess he'd given this shit a lot of thought. It was different for both of us; we had women to protect now. This shit was fucked

None of us were too much into the job after that and it was no surprise when we knocked off right on time. I wanted to get back to my woman and eyeball her to make sure she was okay. I'd put an icepack between her thighs before leaving the house this morning and ordering her to keep her shit iced until it didn't look like she'd been in a knock out bout with the champ. I'm thinking a good tongue fucking when I got through the door might be just the right medicine. Speaking of which, I pulled my phone. She answered on the first ring. "Hey babe, you got any of that cream on your pussy, you know the ointment shit?"

"A little why, you told me to remember?"

"Yeah I know but I'm on my way home and I'm feeling like dessert before dinner, so why don't you go get yourself ready for me huh?" I could see her fucking blush through the phone. How anyone that liked to ride my dick the way she does could still have a shy bone left in her body was beyond me.

"Okay." Damn she sounded like I was fucking her already. I couldn't wait to get my mouth on her shaved smooth pussy. Damn, my dick was leaking already before I even got the key in the ignition. I ended up speeding and hoping no one pulled me over because there was a sure bet I wasn't gonna stop. You'd think it had been days instead of hours since I'd had her, but suddenly I missed her like crazy.

Chapter 8

LOGAN

Since bringing her home my routine has changed up a lot, women will do that to ya. I left the boys as soon as we cleared the gate and headed for home. It had only been about ten minutes since I gave the heads-up, but damn. "Imagine what you could've done with a whole hour." I kicked off my shit kickers and pulled my sweaty shirt off over my head before tackling my jeans.

She was spread out on the bed, naked, pussy glistening because she had started on herself with her fingers; she wasn't allowed to stick anything else in there but me. "Open." My eyes were already glued between her thighs on her hotspot. She opened her legs wider and bent her legs slightly so I could get a better shot of her fingers as they glided into her already slippery pussy. I loved that sound; that wet sound. My mouth watered.

She drew her fingers out and my eyes flew to hers as she pushed them past her lips and sucked. Damn, I almost whimpered at that shit. I took my cock in hand and stroked, getting some pre-cum in my palm for lube. She diddled her clit and her breath hitched as her eyes followed my hand.

I knelt on the bed between her thighs as we watched each other. "Feed me." She fed me her sticky fingers and I reached down for one of her tits with my free hand.

Leaning over, I sucked her tongue into my mouth before moving down to her nipple. Her hand came down and joined mine, stroking my meat to fullness. She was soon pushing my hand away and scooting down on the bed so she could take my cock in her mouth. I loved fucking her face like this with her in submission under me while I kneel over her.

I love to watch her force most of my length into her mouth and try to deep throat my shit. She used one hand to feed my cock into her mouth while fucking herself with the other. I pushed her fingers away and replaced them with mine. She was tight and hot as I added first two then three fingers into her.

My cock twitched but I didn't want in her mouth this time, when I cum I want to be buried balls deep inside her, I was in the mood to breed her, and I knew just how I wanted to do it, the old fashioned way.

"I want you on your knees." She was only too happy to oblige. I helped her get into just the position I wanted, her ass high and chest low. Opening her up I was happy to see she looked much better than this morning, instead of the angry purplish red she was a nice blend of reddish pink. I inhaled the sweet honeysuckle scent of her pussy before letting my tongue come out for a dip.

Her pussy was already talking to me. You know that in and out thing pussies do when they're hungry for cock, like a breathing organism. I thumbed her pussy deep with both thumbs before pulling them out and going back in with my tongue.

I pulled her ass back hard so that it was spread around my face as I buried my tongue in her pussy, sucking up all her juices. I love eating her pussy from behind; her reaction gets me every time.

I hope to fuck no one was walking around out there because she was already starting her shit and I hadn't even given her the tip of my dick yet. When she started riding my face and tearing at the sheets I decided to fuck with her. I used one of my thumbs, still wet from digging inside her hole, to tease her ass.

I used the fingers of the other hand to play with her clit as I tongue fucked her to orgasm with my thumb in her ass. She went off like a shot, filling my mouth with her juices. I didn't wait for her to come down, just reared up behind her, adjusted her ass for deeper pussy penetration, and slid the dick home.

I hit bottom and started to fuck. Her pussy was like an oven, hotter than usual, shit felt fuck awesome as I tried to get my dick past the lining of her stomach.

I don't know what it is about her, but whenever I'm inside her I want to get deeper than I've ever been in anyone else before. It's like I was trying to find a way to meld us together forever or some sappy shit. Reaching around I took both her tits in my hands and squeezed gently, her pussy flexed and juiced. "Ride my cock; like that." She pushed back against my rod, nice and slow at first before speeding up. By the third slide she was slamming herself back on my cock hard enough to shake the bed.

"Baby…"
"Don't stop Lo, it doesn't hurt I promise." Her voice was breathy and sexy as fuck. I'd stopped moving, letting her get her pleasure, but I had to join in the fun. "I'll try not to hurt you." Her harsh movements back and my strong strokes forward soon had us in a nice rhythm. Her poor pussy was going to be sore again. I held onto her tits trying hard to be careful as I fucked into her like a battering ram while she pushed back and wailed.

I imagined my whole length going into her belly over and over and wondered how the fuck she was taking me with her tiny little ass. She on the other hand was acting like she hadn't had dick in a week and rode my shit raw. I felt her body tighten and her head snapped back just before the warmest pussy juice gushed all over my cock. "That's it, cum on my cock like a good girl." I growled in her ear before taking a nip out of it, and that set her off again.

I went in search of that place deep inside her, that rubbery surface with the tight ring that makes my dick hurt so good, her cervix. When I found it I forced my way in, making her screech bloody murder. "I'm going to breed you tonight."

My eyes closed and I fucking roared as I flooded her pussy walls with my seed. "Fuck yeah, ride it out baby." My little naughty debutant was trying to get the last of my jizz inside her by sliding on and off my still stiff pole.

Her body was overly sensitive to my touch, which meant she was in that multi orgasmic phase she gets into sometimes. I kept my dick inside her and let her do her thing until she could stand for me to touch her again.

"You still hungry baby?" She whimpered; that was answer enough. Poor baby she was in heat. I pulled out and turned her over before climbing back between her thighs and guiding my dick back into her with my hand.

Her eyes were glazed over and her mouth hung open as she fought for breath. I stole what little she had left by covering her mouth with mine and feeding her my tongue as I started a nice slow ride in her pussy.

"I love the smell of your sweat Logan.' She sniffed me as I fucked her, that shit was hot and only made my dick twitch inside her. She licked the salty sweat from my skin as she wrapped her legs higher around my waist and tilted her pussy for a harder fuck. "You want more? You want me to do you harder?" She nodded and bit into her lip.

I lifted up so I could see down to where my dick had her pinned to the bed. My long angry pole looked obscene as it sliced into her soft pink flesh. Her bare pussy was plump and sweet the way it wrapped around me, sucking at my meat greedily for my cream. "I'm gonna cum so hard in your pussy babe."

Her body did that shaking shit it does when she's about to have a massive orgasm. That shit only goes to my head and makes me shoot hard as fuck, which I did ten seconds after her pussy went into overdrive.

I nutted so hard I almost put my damn back out. That's that young pussy, young tight and fresh. "I think I'll fuck you for dinner too, I'm in the mood." She squealed and giggled when I went after her neck. It felt so good inside her sperm soaked pussy I figured I'd stay there until my boy felt like playing again.

"You missed me?" I played with the hair around her face. At times like this, when the need had been fed and I could think clearly again, the love I had for her would rise up inside me and choke the shit outta me. "I always miss you Logan."

And then she says something like that, or something equally sweet and I want to give her the fucking world. I hate getting sappy and shit but it makes her eyes light up when I make an ass of myself, and after last night I figure now was as good a time as any to act like a damn sap.

"I love you Gabriella." See, her eyes lit up like the fourth of July and her arms came up and around my shoulders, pulling me in for a kiss. "I love you too." This time was slower than the last. We kept our mouths sealed together as we both moved to our own rhythm. Her soft skin glided across the smooth Egyptian cotton of the sheets as I fucked into her with long deep strokes. Her nails dug into my back as I held her ass in both hands, lifting her onto my cock for each stroke.

"I love the feel of your pussy like this, when my cum is already inside you doing its thing. Tonight I'm gonna fill you to overflowing."

See, fucking sap; her too good pussy is gonna make me stupid yet. We whispered to each other and shared soft touches in between long meaningful kisses. What the fuck? if she wasn't enjoying herself on my dick so much I would've upped the pace, try to get my damn manhood back.

When I came this time, I held her head in my hand as I sucked on her tongue. Her pussy quivered around my cockmeat just as I was emptying my balls inside her again. "I'm not done with you yet. I'ma hit that pussy all night." She howled with laughter the way I knew she would, she loves that kinda talk, the shit tickles her ass.

We spent the whole night in bed until it was time to make the rounds with my brothers. "Sorry you missed dinner baby." I'd just given her the last of my strength with a quick hard fuck against the shower wall. "It was well worth it."

She wrapped her arms around me, as I was about to put my shirt on. Her towel almost slipped and I was contemplating bending her over the bureau for one last shot before my doorbell rang. "Cock blocking fucks." She thought that shit was funny.

"You stay in this house while I'm gone if you wanna talk to Dani call her on the phone." She looked at me like she had something to say but was afraid of my reaction. I'm not too fond of that look. "Speak." I ran my hand over her hair before kissing her forehead.

"Nothing, it's just, Dani's right across the way, why can't I go see her?"

"Because when I leave I'm putting this place on lockdown and I'm sure Connor's doing the same. I don't know what the fuck is gonna go down tonight, but I know when I get back I want you in my bed waiting. Now kiss your man so he can go do what he gotta do."

She didn't argue with me this time, and she had a point. It made sense to leave the two women together, but you never give your enemy a sitting target. If anyone came here, not that there was a chance in hell they'd get past our security measures, but just in case, they won't know where to hit and that might buy us time.

Chapter 9

LOGAN

Tonight was the night the ship was supposedly coming in and we'd done all we could to secure the area, but we'll see what we see. I wasn't sure that they would show with everything else that was going on. There was way too much going on at once if you ask me though, and it was never too good to have too many irons in too many fires at once.

"I have the sneaky suspicion after that call that these fucks are gonna be even more careful than before. They know we're onto them now, I'm not feeling too hopeful about tonight." I made the announcement when I stepped out the door to my waiting entourage of pains in the ass.

When we'd conversed with Robert and the other misfits last time this was the date they'd given us for the pick up. Now with the money gone, and them knowing who knows what, since we had to wait for Vanessa to bring Rosalind in to tell us what she'd told them, we were just going just in case.

They'd be dumb fucks if they showed up tonight and we'd already decided they weren't that. We know they hadn't made the move already because we'd been keeping an eye out.

"Damn Lo, give it a rest already, you're getting as bad as Connor, damn." They were all trying hard not to grin behind their hands. "What the fuck are you talking about Ty?" Like I didn't know, even when we were in the trenches these fucks were always talking shit, nosy fucks.

"Took a long nap did you brother?" Quinn can be part ass too when he wants to be, but I chose to ignore them all as we moved towards our bikes. "I don't know what you're talking about." I hopped on my ride and waited for the rest of the gossip committee to do the same. "You never turned the lights on buddy, it doesn't take a rocket scientist to figure out since no SEAL worth his salt would take a fucking nap in the evening."

"Fuck you, fuck all of you, except maybe you Con." That was only because he got as much shit as I did.

"He's the one who started it." I gave Con the stink eye after Zak's announcement, but he held up his hand like he was innocent, somehow I didn't believe him, could be the smirk he was trying hard but failing to hide. I guess it's true what they say, misery loves company and his ass was tired of being the only one.

We did our thing, easing down to the street before the boardwalk, lights out. We left our rides in one of their hiding places, we never leave them in the same place all the time, too easy. There was no one around, the town was literally asleep and had been for a while now. There were distant lights farther away, probably porch lights and shit, but closer to the water there was nothing but dark.

"Feel how peaceful that is." It's one of those nights where the sky is a blanket of dark blue velvet, barely a star to be seen, no other brightness, but the light of the moon reflecting off the water. I could sit here with my girl and enjoy the cool breeze on a warm summer night, if some fuck wasn't using my spot to run his illegal shit.

The shots came from above and went wide. My men were in motion already, as we hit the ground. "Are you fucking kidding me?" I didn't have to speak, just with hand motions I sent Zak and Tyler around and behind where the shots had came from. The rest of us crawled on our bellies towards the boardwalk, staying in the bushes, guns drawn.

The shooter was on a side angle to the water, which means we were heading to cover but would still be in a position to take the fucker out if the others didn't get them. "Alive." I uttered the word into the watch I had on my wrist that doubled as a communication device.

There was another spate of gunfire, which seemed not to be aimed anywhere in particular, unless you were laying down fire to subdue. I looked at the others like 'what the fuck!'

"Who the fuck do they have out there, Barney Fife?" There came the sound of running feet and tussling, followed by an expletive and a few thumps. Zak came striding back with a gift, which he thoughtfully dropped at my feet. What the fuck is this?" It was a damn kid.

"Who the fuck? What are you doing out here kid?" The boy couldn't be more than seventeen, shaking like a leaf with terror in his eyes. I would feel sorry for his little ass if he hadn't just taken shots at me.

"Were you the one shooting?" he nodded and looked around like he was about to shit himself. "Why?" I cold practically hear the kid's bones rattling together.
"They told me to."
"They, who's they?" I knew what he was gonna say even before he formed the words in his damn mouth. I'm tired of chasing fucking ghosts. I'm especially tired of coming up against this shit over and over with no results. "I don't know sir, they didn't say." My men were keeping their eyes peeled to the surrounding area while we had our little chat, but it was like I said, they weren't dumb enough to show up here tonight.

"You don't know them but yet you came out here in the middle of the night to take shots at me and my men because they asked you to." He started shaking harder and looking for an escape route of which there was none. Ty was looking at him like he wanted to put one in him and the others were in position to block all routes of escape.

"They said they would hurt us if I didn't, I swear sir I didn't know what else to do, that's why I shot wide, I didn't really want to hurt anyone. They tried telling me that it was part of some night raid game, but I knew better, I've seen stuff on TV ya know." Now he was babbling.

"Kid what the fuck are you talking about?" he opened his mouth to speak but I held my hand up for silence. "Start at the beginning." He wiped under his nose and tried to compose himself. I saw myself at his age and my heart gave a little. That shit was dangerous as fuck, you never identify with the enemy, no matter where or who, but there was something about the kid.

"Okay, my friends and I were messing around down here a few months ago. We weren't supposed to be, but we thought it was fun to hide out here and steal a few smokes. These guys came, they didn't know we were here at first and we didn't even hear what they were talking about at first I swear. But when they noticed us they went ape shit. It was really scary when they put on the things on their faces and came after us."

"What things on their faces?" Was this kid reciting a movie to me or some shit? He looked from me to the others and down at the sand and brush. "Those military mask things they wear in the movies." I looked at my brothers over his head as he carried on with his story. "They were scary enough to begin with, but when they put those on it was like one of those horror movies you know. Then they roughed us up a little, not much, they just wanted to know what we heard. Then they asked our names and I was so stupid I gave them the right information, my friends didn't though; they were smart." He wiped his nose again.

"Have you ever seen these guys before?" He squinted in thought and shrugged his shoulders before looking out at the water.

"Maybe, that night I thought one of them looked familiar but it wasn't his face, it was the way he moved ya know, I don't know how to explain it. There aren't that many bodybuilder types around here ya know, so he kinda stuck out. I know they're not from around here though and when I asked the Commander if his friends were doing some kind of training here in town he seemed surprised." Well fuck that changes things now didn't it?

"You knew the commander?" Everyone was paying attention now, as the kid seemed to relax a little, sensing that just maybe his stupid ass might make it out of this alive.

"Yeah, Don, he was a cool old guy, but when I asked him I could tell he didn't know what I was talking about and then he asked me all these questions, kinda like what you're doing now. Then he got real quiet like and I don't think he was too happy." He did that sniffling shit again, reminding me of his youth. "Go on, what else did the commander do?"

"He played it down ya know, the way adults do when they wanna keep something from us kids, but I knew it was something big because he seemed deep in thought when he told me to head on home and stay away from the boardwalk for a little while at night, but he sure did ask a lotta questions, like a lot. I wish I'd got a better look at the guys' faces but I didn't, I couldn't even describe the tattoos because it was dark and they were partly hidden under their sleeves, but I think they might've been the same."

"And you say this happened a year or so ago?" He got sad and picked at the grass before nodding his head and looking at me for the first time. "Yeah, just a few months before Don died.' I didn't like how the way he said that shit made me feel, and from the restless movement around me no one else did either.

The commander had supposedly suffered a heart attack out on his boat; fuck me no. I looked at my brothers and barely contained the rage that was just beneath the surface. The same question was reflected in their eyes and the winds had just shifted.

I questioned the kid some more until he gave up all he had. "How did they talk you into this, how did they find you?"
"They knew my name, just looked my family up in the phonebook I guess. They told me it was a game and that the bullets weren't real, they were these new type of bullets that the army

was trying out or something like that, but I knew it was a lie, because when I practiced the cat died."

Fucking kid started crying, what the fuck was this shit? I let him get it out of his system before going on to tell me how he was contacted by phone, how the package was left for him a few days ago and how they convinced his dumb ass to do it. Apparently he wasn't as dumb as he looked because he'd shot wide and long.

"Why you, why did they choose you for their little experiment?" "Because I'm the best marksman on my reserves team I guess, and because they knew that if I didn't do it they'd tell my mom what I'd been up to down here a year ago and she'd skin me." Something was off as fuck, why would obvious professionals send a kid to take shots at us?

"Fuck let's move." I grabbed the kid and we high tailed it out of there just before the place went to shit. The explosion was loud and lit up the night sky like fireworks, hopefully most of the town's folks would think that that's what it was.

The whole fucking boardwalk and a good chunk of the beach was gone. "Fuckers used C4. Ty clean him up." The kid puked himself and I didn't even wanna know what that smell was that was coming from him. "Fuck outta here, little shit took shots at us let him wallow in his shit." I gave him a glare which he ignored as we watched the night sky light up. "Fine, he's on the back of your ride, let's get the fuck outta here before the brigade shows up." He grumbled some shit before collaring the kid and heading for the water.

I wasn't surprised when I heard the splash and the loud complaint from the kid. They met us back at the bikes and Ty was contemplating tying the kid behind his bike and dragging him back, fucking nut job.

We headed back keeping to the side streets with our lights out. This shit had just taken a turn. All the implications the kid made had my radar on high fucking alert. Military, it sounded like military, but which branch, who and why?

It was definitely no newbies running this shit; it was too organized, too secretive. And the way they went after us tonight, took someone with a head on his shoulder and balls. One thing I wasn't dwelling on too hard, not yet anyway, not until I've had a chance to talk it over with my brothers. The commander had suspected something, and then the commander had died. I'm gonna have a fuck storm on my hands of my suspicions turned out to be true, we're gonna have to do some serious digging in the next few days.

The kid was scared when we clanged the big ass gates shut behind us, locking him in. I could kinda see why the town folk were so interested in what was going on behind these walls.

First, the shits were higher than regulation, but we pulled a few strings and got shit taken care of. The gates were special made titanium, wasn't shit getting through there for all that we'd had them designed to look normal and not like the military grade shit they really were. There was no way too see in from the outside, and the houses were situated in such a way that no one knew exactly where each structure was. Add the fact that the walls were reinforced with a material that prohibited any kind of radar and we were sitting in fucking Knox. This is the reason for leaving the girls home and not letting them go to work or anywhere else. They were safer here than anywhere else.

Chapter 10

LOGAN

Back at the compound we all headed for the commander's place without question. It was the first time since the night we'd buried him that we were going in like this. Even when our homes were being built we preferred to sleep outside in tents than to invade his territory, but somehow this felt right.

I knew from their somber moods that we were all on the same wavelength. I just needed the kid to tell me what he knew and what if anything he could remember from back then.

I didn't lift the shields on my house yet and neither did Con, until we were in there with eyes on their asses I don't think either of us were gonna feel comfortable doing that. It wasn't a small thing that we were shot at tonight, I knew our blood was still up, which meant Gaby's pussy was in for a workout again, damn. I'm gonna owe her and she's probably gonna try to hit me up with this wedding shit again, fuck.

We headed for the study and Con went right for the liquor, which was right where the old man had left it on the sidebar. Each man nodded yes to his silent offer and he poured seven snifters of cognac. "Sit." I pointed at the kid who was looking around at us in awe.

"He told me about you guys." His eyes went around the room and I'm sure the granite looks in my brothers' faces was probably making him shit in his drawers. "The commander talked to you about us?" My voice was more frightening than disbelieving I think, as he swallowed and his eyes snapped back to me.

"Some, no top secret stuff or anything, he just always told me that you were stand up guys and if I was ever in trouble…that's kinda why I couldn't shoot you you know, because I know he liked you guys and he was a good guy, so you must be good guys too right."

He fidgeted in his chair when there was nothing forthcoming, but all our minds were working. The commander would never discuss our missions, but he wasn't big about talking about us period except to a select few.

There was another shared look before I answered the kid again. "Why didn't you come to us then?" He looked back over his shoulder again before scooting forward in his chair with a whisper.

"I think they're watching me, my house I mean, and my phone sounds funny. I would've come I promise, but I didn't want to risk it. I don't even know what I'm supposed to do now that I've botched it." He looked miserable the little fuck and I as reminded that he'd puked and shit himself not long ago. "Get the kid some clothes." I directed it to Cord who was the one most likely to adhere seeing as how the kid had shot at us and the rest of them were an unforgiving bunch. He didn't look too pleased by my request either though. "He looks fine to me the little fuck."

"Cord!" Sometimes my brothers make me tired, all of them. I threw back my cognac and rested my head against the chair back. "Fine, but he gets any of his shit on my clothes I'll skin his ass."

He marched out of the room his massive shoulders straight, feet stomping. The kid must be scared shitless surrounded by all this testosterone. But instead he seemed amazed, just what the fuck had the commander told him anyway?

"There's a little bathroom down the hall go clean up."

"I know where it is." That got a few raised eyebrows. The commander never let anyone in his place as far as we knew, but it seemed he and this kid were close. "I wonder why the old guy never told us about this kid?"

"Probably never had time. Remember we were supposed to come out and then we got called away?" Devon was pacing back and forth, I wasn't worried about him though, I kept my eye on Ty and gave Con the look that had him moving closer to our problem child.

"Yeah, and he'd said it was urgent, we just put it down to his health after he passed but what if it was about all this?"

When the glass hit the unlit fireplace mantle I wasn't surprised. I knew it wouldn't take long for everyone to start putting the pieces

together and coming up with stink.
"Con."
"Got him." He moved to crows Tyler against the wall while the others moved into position just in case shit went south. I heard Cord returning and called out to him. "Keep the kid out Cord we're dealing with Ty." His 'fuck' told me he got it; I didn't have to explain.

"Murder, they fucking killed him the spineless fucks. I'm gonna cut off their heads and piss down their motherfucking throats before this is done." There was wet in his eyes which I knew with Ty was as dangerous as it gets. Next he'll go cold, just flat cold and heaven help us if he reaches that stage because there isn't fuck any of us can do if he does. "Ty, we don't know that…"

"Fuck that Cap. Military mask, the kid tells the commander, the old man starts digging the old man dies. Didn't we all question his death in the beginning? Didn't we all comment on how strange it was that he'd died from a heart attack when he'd been healthy as an ox the last time we saw him? And we let him down.

They fucking killed him and we built fucking houses and went on like nothing happened." I saw the change come into him then, his whole body locked down and his fucking eyes went dead. Con stepped away because he knew the signs. Our boy was here but gone.

"And there he goes, fucking ice." Con looked over his shoulder at my words with that look of resignation he gets whenever his dog pops his leash. "Don't worry Con we'll all keep an eye on him." Fuck me I need this shit.

***

We couldn't let the kid go home yet so after we'd questioned him some more and were all coming down from our adrenaline high, we headed for our respective homes. Cord surprisingly enough, volunteered to put the kid up for the night.

Ty hadn't said fuck one after his outburst, which meant I had a powder keg on my hands, and the only thing keeping the general population safe thus far was the fact that we didn't know who the fuck.

"Logan." Her soft whisper smoothed out some of the rough edges as I kicked off my shoes and shed my clothes. I climbed into bed and pulled her into my arms.

"I need you baby." There were no words exchanged between us, I went straight for the pussy. I pushed the sheets away from her sleep warm body and dove right in with my tongue. She wasn't allowed to wear anything in my bed except one of my old t-shirts, but definitely no panties, I liked knowing my fingers and anything else was just a slip away from her entrance, no barriers.

I lifted her onto my tongue and growled into her pussy as her taste flooded my senses. She was already moving like a wanton, her nails digging into my scalp. "Ohhh Logan, please."

Damn, greedy bitch never lets me get my fill of pussy juice before she starts her shit. A nice hard slap on her ass was no help; that shit only made her wilder. "Yes, spank my ass." This little girl is an enigma she can go from zero to fifty in the blink of an eye.

I pulled my tongue out her snatch before she scalped my ass and flipped her over none too gently. She was ready for me, canting her ass just at the right angle for the dick to go in. I hit her spot with the first stroke and she sprung a leak.

"Oh fuck yeah, tight hot pussy." We were both gone, I was working off whatever the fuck was going on in my head and I'm guessing she'd been having sweet dreams or some shit because her pussy was hungry as fuck. She was taking me in deeper than usual at this angle and my dick was a happy camper, I hit the rubbery surface of her cervix and that's where the fun begun.

Her scream was more like a growl and her body shook uncontrollably as she spasm all over my cock. I wasn't even close to finished, so I let her ride her shit out before fucking into her hard again, over and over.

"I'm going to fuck your pussy raw, then I'm gonna eat you 'til you cum again and again." That set her off again and she squeezed my cock. I pulled out and latched my mouth onto her pussy so I could drink from her.

She rode my face as I ate her out from behind, before kneeling behind her and slamming home. "Ugh, Logan, so deep." She arched her back and pushed he ass back, spreading her legs wider to take more of me. I like this shit. The sheets were literally torn off the bed as we fucked each other and I still hadn't cum.

It was going to take me a while; it usually does when I get like this. When she wound down from her third or fourth orgasm I pulled out and put her on her back with her legs over my shoulders and her pussy tilted up for the dick.

My dick was extra hard as pre-cum dripped down onto her pussy lips. I opened her cunt with my thick cockhead and slid in nice and slow, feeding her half my dick while she whimpered and moaned. "I'm going into your belly." I warned her one-second before fucking the rest of my dick into her. She was bent double with her arms pinned above her head, total submission. I attacked her tits with my teeth next, leaving my mark behind as I suckled her hard, going from one plump nipple to the next.

My dick bored into her like a battering ram as I fucked out my frustration and anger in her. She stayed with me every step of the way letting me know she wanted to be fucked hard.

She did some kind of gymnastics with her pussy and put a crimp in my shit. "Fuck!" I came like a fountain in her pussy and damn near killed her as I pounded out my lust on her poor little body.

I let her legs drop, but I didn't pull out, just laid on top of her with our lips locked together and my dick dripping the last of his offerings inside her deep wet cavern. I didn't want to leave her and she wouldn't let me go, so we stayed like that until we started fucking again, into the early morning light.

Chapter 11

CONNOR

I woke to a strange sound and hit the floor running when I realized what it was. My heart was in my lungs and I was already breaking out in a cold sweat.

"Danielle, baby, what the fuck?" I barely got the words past the fear lump in my chest. I moved towards her slowly, not sure what the fuck I was supposed to do. I'd never seen her SICK. I knelt on the cold hard marble of the bathroom floor where she was already sitting leaned over the toilet.

"Did I hurt you last night?" I tried to replay everything I'd done in my head, I hadn't been any rougher than in times past. Yes I was a little fucked up because of what we were beginning to suspect about the commander's death, but I wouldn't have hurt her.

She was shaking her head and holding her tummy, looking green as fuck. She used the last of her strength it looked like, to flush the toilet, before I picked her up. I helped her get cleaned up and she just folded into me with her head on my chest.

I held her there with a hand behind her head while I tried to understand what was going on. I hurt because she hurt, but in a few seconds I was gonna switch to pissed if I didn't get some answers. Not pissed at her of course, but pissed at some fuck. I take good care of her so she doesn't get sick. I load her up on natural vitamin C and shit.

"Baby talk to me please; what's going on?" I felt her head and neck but she wasn't hot. She fucking groaned like I'd twat punched her and sent my ass into panic. "Connor, don't move so much." What the fuck, I wasn't moving. I shushed her the best I could and lifted her in my arms.

"I'm taking you to the doctor." I laid her on the bed and had to count to ten before I could get myself under control. She looked pitiful. Her skin was clammy to the touch and she grabbed her tummy and did that groaning shit again.

"No Connor please, I don't need the doctor. Just let me lay here for a little bit and I'll be fine I promise." Her voice didn't sound like she was going to be fine and I wanted to yell and scream like a little bitch.

When she started crying I was done. I climbed onto the bed as easily as I could and tried taking her in my arms but she balked. "What the fuck." I pulled my phone and sent out an S.O.S to my brothers, this was some team shit. I remembered to cover her up in time as I heard their feet running from all directions outside. They came through the door like they were expecting an invasion.

"What is it, what's wrong?" Of course Logan led the charge. Cord had the kid there with him and at my raised brow he sent him out of the room.

"Go wait out there kid." He pointed to the general area of the living room. "You leave this house the lion Connor keeps in the backyard will eat your scrawny ass." The kid bleated like he really believed that shit.

"I don't know what's wrong she's sick." I think I was about to fucking cry. Last night when I came in she'd been asleep. I'd been out of my head a little I admit, what with Tyler going off the rails before I could reel him in, and thinking that these humps had ended the old man. It was a lot to take in all at once.

So when I came to bed and pulled her under me, I may have been a little more than she's used to. I replayed the first, second and third time I fucked her and couldn't see where I'd fucked up. Could it have been when I had her on her hands and knees? That was the last time and I was the roughest then I think, but only because her pussy fucking owns me when we're in that position and all I can think about is getting deeper inside her.

But she was right there with me, egging me on, begging me to do her harder, faster. Now my brothers were standing in my fucking bedroom looking at my dying woman because I was such a fucking pig. I wanted to tear the hair from my head, but I couldn't move because it seemed any kind of movement hurt her.

Gaby came rushing into the room with her hair still wet and her shirt buttoned all wrong and shit. Lo tried to snag her but she evaded his ass and headed for the bed. Dani picked up her head and looked at her and the two women shared some kind of look that us men didn't know what the fuck.

They reached out to each other and Gaby climbed on the bed on the other side of her and took her hand. "Careful, don't shake the bed." I didn't even look at Lo to see what the fuck was going on with him. Brother or not, I'm pretty sure he wasn't too pleased to see his woman on a bed with another dude no matter what the circumstances. "Okay everybody out, you too Connor" I gave Logan a look after his woman had lost her damn mind.

"Bro, handle your shit." I love Gabriella and all but she's fucked if she thinks I'm leaving my woman like this. He started calling her over. "Babe come on, get outta there." She just looked at all of them lined off in my bedroom as if ready for battle. Ty was looking pissed as fuck like he just needed an excuse, any excuse to start blasting some shit. Dani started that groaning shit and then the two of them started whispering to each other. "Gabriella swear to fuck, if you know what's wrong with her you better tell me."

"Con."

"Fuck that Lo, if she knows…" Gaby leaned over and whispered in my ear. I didn't mean to jump off the bed.

I pointed my finger at Dani who was looking close to tears. "You're with child? You're going to be uncles." I was in a state of shock when I turned to my brothers with the news. It took their thick asses a minute to get it before the backslapping and congratulations kicked in. I turned back to her and knelt next to the bed this time.

I'd heard stories about morning sickness; apparently this shit was vicious. "I'm sorry Connor." She was a mess.

"What, why?" I was a little slow it seemed because I had no idea what she was talking about, why would she be sorry? If she...no asshole don't go there. "Because you weren't ready I thought..."

"Shh, shh, of course I'm ready, I told you so didn't I?" Gaby climbed off the bed and headed for the door, but I wasn't paying her or the others any mind. "Come on boys let's go find something to eat." They all left the room, but Ty was soon back with a Ginger ale. "Gaby said this should work for now." He was whispering like we were in church.

I was still kneeling at the side of the bed with her hand in mine, not sure what to do next. I wanted to be inside her again, that's what I wanted, I don't know why the urge, the need was so strong. I helped her sit up to sip her drink, and miraculously she seemed to transform after a few sips of the shit. "You okay now? I'm gonna have to have a talk with my son about this making his mama sick business." I smiled to try to ease the tension in my chest before placing the almost empty can down on the nightstand.

We sat like that for a while whispering to each other as the news sunk in that I was going to be a father. "Is this real baby, you're sure?" She nodded her reassurance against my chest that was already swelling with pride.

I told her about all the things I was going to do with my son. All the things his uncles and I were gonna teach him. She was looking and sounding better already, and my dick was on the hunt. Looked like she had the same idea too.

"Do you think you can do me real soft so the others won't hear?" She nibbled my fucking ear. What the fuck was she carrying in there, Damien? She was like a whole new person. I looked from her to the door and back before going over to close and lock it.

She pulled her nightgown, my t-shirt, off over her head and laid back with her legs spread. I didn't know what the fuck, but I was going with it. "No don't Connor, just come inside me, I need you inside me." She wouldn't let me warm her up. "Fine." I wasn't sure about this shit but I went with it because that seemed like the thing to do in this situation.

I just simply pushed my boxers down and released my cock to slip inside her. She was warm and wet but I didn't have time to think about how the fuck she got that way because her pussy grabbed me and sucked me in. I couldn't pound fuck her the way I wanted to because of my son, and because of the six nosy fucks inside my kitchen.

"Fuck baby, your pussy's hot." Damn I never felt anything that good in my life, hot, wet pussy. I stroked into her nice and soft as she dug her nails into my ass. We had to keep our voices low and so I buried my face in her neck, closer to her ear. "Does that feel good lil mama?" She pushed her pussy harder onto my dick and moaned into my neck.

"Yeah clench that pussy for me. I want to feel you cum on my dick." Her body grew hot and her pussy gushed. "I'm gonna fuck you all day, they're gonna need a crowbar to get me out this pussy." I was on some sort of high I realized. I was going to be a dad, me and Dani had made a baby. Fuck, just the thought had my sap rising. I ground into her harder, lifting her leg around my hip to open her up more for my long dick. She was taking me like a champ this morning, her pussy nice and pliable.

"Fuck I'm cumming already, cum with me." I made sure she did by placing my hand between us and circling her clit with my thumb. I had to catch her scream in my mouth when she went off and bathed my cock again. My eyes crossed and my back locked up as I emptied what felt like a gallon of my seed inside her. "Yes Connor, fuck me." Oh shit.

Chapter 12

LOGAN

I stood off to the side and watched her with my arms folded as she puttered around Connor and Dani's kitchen. I gave each one of the ungrateful fucks sitting at the table the death glare to let them know there will be consequences if they made her feel bad about her cooking. I wasn't sure what she could do in the kitchen since she'd been playing it shy up until now, but whichever way it went these fucks had better not hurt her feelings or I'll shoot their asses.

"Ty you fuck sit down." He was hovering like a starving orphan. At least he wasn't looking like murder central any longer, shoulda known his greedy ass would be like this. He just grinned at me like a simpleton but I wasn't sure I trusted that shit either. The kid was acting like he was stuck to Cord's side and my brother for once wasn't trying to get away, weird. He caught me looking and shrugged. "Kid's got brains, you should see what he can do with a piece." I just lifted my brow at him but he interpreted that shit easily enough.

"I wasn't worried about him trying anything, I could snap his neck without blinking." The kid swallowed hard and I realized I didn't even know his name.

"Did you get a name at least while you two were bonding?" what the fuck was going on around here anyway? "Davey. His family lives in that little pink and blue house on the edge of town."

We'd all seen the place, who could miss it? There was a garden out front that looked as big as the place itself, and though the place was sagging a bit, the general upkeep was good. It was the unusual color in the middle of all the other brick houses that made it stand out though, and gave the impression that some very unique people lived there.

"Your parents gonna come looking for you?"
"Ma'll be at work, she leaves early so she probably doesn't know I never made it home, but sis might." That seemed to scare him a little. "Afraid of your sister are you?" He nodded as his eyes went towards the platter of pancakes my woman was bringing to the table.

"Fuck that smells good." I forgot all about the kid and his fear of his sister as I watched the others fall on the cakes like hungry wolves.

"Oh fuck, you've been holding out." Tyler gave me the stink eye as Zak reached for a couple to plop on his own plate. "I bet Lo the fuck knew she could do this." He closed his eyes and sighed as he chewed on the buttermilk pecan pancake. I was smiling like a proud papa at her and she beamed from ear to ear. She didn't need words to tell her how they felt about her cooking, the grunts and groans not to mention Devon stabbing Quinn in the hand with his fork when he reached for the last one on the plate was enough.

"Here you go Davey, I was wondering what you were doing here. Susie knows where you are?" she sat the kid and gave him his own plate. "What the fuck, where's mine?"

She patted my cheek like an imbecile and grinned, she was full of herself because the boys liked her shit. "I saved the best for last." I stood at the stove while she poured more batter onto the griddle and then pulled a shitload of bacon out of the broiler. "Ty sit the fuck down." Geez this fucker and food!

Con and Dani soon joined us and she wasn't looking so green anymore, in fact she had a nice glow about her and Con was looking like king of the walk. Fucking douche interrupted my morning session but it looked like he'd not missed out. Fuck there's going to be a baby. I walked over to my brother and hugged him.

"Congratulations bro this shit is amazing." The others soon joined in and the talk turned to babies and all the shit they were gonna need, and my eyes went to my woman as I imagined her round with my child. My dick sprung up and leaked. I was tempted to drag her outta there but shit turned into a mini celebration.

Con held Dani on his lap like he was afraid to let her go and Ty and Zak teased her about blowing up like a whale soon. Even the kid was grinning and smiling like he was part of the crew and for a little while there, we weren't thinking about the shit storm that was about to unfold.

I let them enjoy the last bit of happiness before we had to get back to the trenches. The kid was another extra worry, now that he'd done his part, I didn't know what the fucks had planned for him, so I couldn't just cut him loose. I would've left him with the girls, but with Dani pregnant that was a fucking no-no. If the kid even sneezed wrong Con would cap his ass.

In the end we headed back to the commander's place and had the kid call his sister and give her some story about leaving early. With that squared away we got down to business trying to piece shit together.

We hadn't heard any sirens until long after we'd come back last night, so chances are no one had seen us leaving the area in such a hurry. I was half expecting a phone call any second, unless they thought we were brainless assholes who had fallen for their trick.

"I think last night was more of a warning than anything else. They couldn't have believed that we'd be that fucking stupid." We had the kid in front of the TV with headphones on so he couldn't hear what we were discussing. Although it seems he was tight the with old man, he was still an unknown and there was no way I was gonna trust him with shit. As long as he was here there were going to be eyes and ears on him at all times.

"Maybe, but we can't sit around and wait for them to try again. From everything the kid said we know the commander was onto something." Con was going through the ledger again interpreting what was written there and breaking down the code.

So far we knew that the kid had brought the situation to the commander and he in turn had picked up the scent. There was definitely a military presence involved, but so far all the old man had written about was speculation. But he was convinced that someone very high up was involved.

"It looks like he was digging for a while guys, and knowing him, he would've been asking questions. He would've been smart about it, but if that got back to the wrong ears it could be why they killed him, if they killed him."

Connor looked at Ty who was already getting restless again. "We're gonna take this shit one thing at a time. First we have to decide what to do with this kid, he can't stay here indefinitely and we can't just cut him loose."

"His parents won't mind if he stays here with us, we'll just come up with a story, tell them we're taking him under our wing." I gave Cord my 'what the fuck' look because he was acting like one of the pod people. "Come again, since when do you wanna babysit?" Every mission we ever had that involved getting some diplomat's brat out of shit, he was the first to grouch about babysitting. Now he's acting like it's the most natural thing in the world to take on this kid.

"Look, all I'm saying is that from listening to him last night, we can work it. It's not that they don't care, but they need a break, that sister of his sounds like a real handful, maybe we'll be helping them out.

Besides, they know he was cool with the commander and he says he spent a lot of time here before the old man died, so it's worth a try." Huh, I'm not sure what the fuck but whatever. I shrugged my answer and went back to looking through the old man's belongings for anything else that might help us.

The women were at my house today and the place was on lock. We'd given the workers the day off; they can have a long weekend. Thank fuck the job was all but done and only needed the cosmetic finishes before we handed it over. One less thing to worry about.

Just as I expected, the phone rang with the same unknown bullshit as before. "Yeah." I motioned to the others and the place went quiet except for the squeaking of the chair the kid was swiveling around on as he watched cartoons.

"Sorry we missed you last night, until next time. You can consider that a pre-warning, next time we won't be so generous."
"Is that what that was, you army boys have a lot to learn. There were holes so wide in your little scheme my brothers and I walked right through them. It wasn't even as good as a made for TV movie plot. And who uses kids to do their dirty work, what are you a bitch?" Come on asshole lose some of that control.

"Listen you seadog, that will be the day when one of you could get one over on us. You think you can outsmart me, better men than you have tried. Stay out of our business or next time one of your women will get it, or are they trained as well?" His laughter rang out as he hung up. I took the phone away and hit replay again. "Did that fuck just threaten my pregnant woman?" Ah shit, fucking tunnel vision.

"Con keep it together, the girls are safe as long as they stay inside you know that. We have to figure out what the fuck we're dealing with and do it fast though because they're not gonna wanna stay cooped up for long."

I know Gabriella and her wedding shit is gonna be a problem, but I couldn't worry about that now. "He's army, no marine would refer to anyone as a seadog and the air force is full of elitist dicks who wouldn't know what to do with this shit. If they were navy the commander would've sniffed it out, so I'm going with army."

"Fine but that still doesn't tell us who what or why?" Ty got up from his chair to pace as the others all looked to me for answers. "That's where the power of deduction comes into play. We need to find out what base is near here, who's running it and get the dynamics of the place, the ins and outs so to speak. It would be perfect if we could get someone on the inside that don't have a clue what the fuck we're up to, so we could have eyes inside."

"We could offer some sap a weekend job or some shit, maybe a reserve, then work on him. Nah, that'll take time." Ty was thinking on his feet as were the rest of us, but we all knew it wasn't going to be that easy.

"Vanessa is supposed to be here with the Rosalind woman tonight, let's see what we can get out of her. In the meantime let's get to work." Before we could get started on anything the buzzer for the main gate went off. Everyone turned to look at everyone else. "Who's expecting a delivery?" Everyone shook their heads including me. "Who the fuck?" Quinn pulled it up on the computer and panned the area.

"Shit, that's my sister, that's Susie." This kid was really afraid of his sister. I couldn't see why, she looked like about a hundred pounds and she was about a good two inches shorter than her brother, who looked like he was about to shit himself. "I'll get her."

Cord was out of his seat and headed for the door. What the fuck were we supposed to do with all these unknowns running around? The rest of us headed out at a slower pace with the kid bringing up the rear. If he was gonna hang around someone was gonna have to help him find a pair.

"Listen asshole I want to see my brother, until I see for myself that he's okay I'm not moving. Now get the hell out my way before I call the cops." Cord was standing arms crossed, legs braced in front of the pint size pixie with the behemoth attitude. "I said move dickhead." His eyes went wide when she poked him in the chest. The rest of us just stood back and watched while her brother groaned.

"I'm okay Susie, I'm right here." He moved out from behind us so she could see him, and see that we hadn't mauled him or whatever the fuck it is that she'd expected.

The girls heard the commotion and peeped out the window but knew better than to step foot outside without getting the all clear. Cord's gruff voice brought me back to the situation that was going on around me.

"And I said you're not getting by until I search you, now turn your little ass around and head out, you've annoyed me." I'm pretty sure everyone else had the same dumbfounded look on their face that I did. I've never heard Cord be anything but courteous to a female before, usually he's their biggest champion. The kid started to move forward but Quinn pulled him back. "Stay out of it."

The two in front of us squared off like two warheads, she was breathing fire and he looked like…what the fuck? I had to change tactics and take her in again. Okay, she was about five one five two tops, wild chestnut colored curls that seemed to go in every direction, and cat green eyes.

Her skin was that porcelain shit that people write about and if her little nose turned up any higher it'll touch her brow. "Are you seeing what I'm seeing?" I asked Connor out the side of my mouth so the kid didn't hear me, and especially to keep it away from Ty. I might be wrong, but I was pretty sure I wasn't.

"Yep, if Ty catches on there's gonna be hell to pay. Then again it might distract him from plotting mayhem." That's a thought. Now I

know all my men, down to their little
peccadillos and if I were not mistaken
I would swear my brother was fighting
a serious case of lust. It was the way
he was holding his body, the way he
was scolding her yet protecting her
from the rest of us.

That's Cord's thing when it
comes to a woman he's topping. I've
never seen it look this intense before
though, and never with someone he
hadn't already taken to his bed.

"Try it shit for brains and I will
kick you in your nuts so hard you'd
have 'em for breakfast."
"Geez Susie would you quit it? You
see I'm fine, now go on home and I'll
be there later." She withered him with
a look but it seemed all her venom was
reserved for Cord. Ty the nosy fuck
came to stand beside me and from the
way he was squinting I knew he was
onto something. "Well fuck Cap, is it
the water? What the fuck?" He
hightailed it back to his place, the

jackass, while I got the others back on track.

"Alright the rest of you, break it up, we've got shit to do."
"Is that what I think it is?" Quinn pointed his chin at Cord and the female who were now in each other's face."
"Looks like."
"Fuck, Ty's right, I maybe should look into getting some sort of repellant. How long did it take this one?" Devon started backing away like he thought the shit was catching.

"Far as I can tell this is the first time they've met."
"Well shit." that was Zak's pithy parting shot and I didn't even want any part of his fuckery.

"Come on kid, looks like you're with me for the duration." I looked back at the two of them and felt almost sorry for the female. If Cord had he scent she was in for it, that brother is a

controlling fuck if I ever met one.
"How old is your sister again?"
"Twenty-one why?" he looked back at
them but I put my hand on his shoulder
and dragged him off to my house.

At least she was legal because
chances are from what I'd just seen out
there, it wasn't going to be long before
she was topped. Damn, maybe Ty the
fuck was onto something, maybe there
was something in the water.

Chapter 13

LOGAN

The day had been long and the night promised to be longer. Cord was the main attraction, he and the female that was caught between shooting daggers at him with her eyes, and mooning over him, that shit was making my teeth hurt.

The kid had proven himself to be more of a bottomless pit than Ty, by eating me out of house and home all afternoon, while the women fawned all over him like he was three. Connor was understandably preoccupied with his woman and their unborn child, and we'd already had a meeting, all of us, about the need to protect them at all cost.

Security was beefed up and Connor was working on getting her to stay home until we got shit squared away. I knew Gabriella was gonna give me shit, but I was gonna insist she stay her little ass put too. We were taking a break and every man was off doing his own thing.

Cord had taken his new shadows with him and I was alone with my woman. Things were gonna be a little hectic around here for the next few days, and I needed her cooperation.

"Babe I'm sorry, but you're gonna either have to put your wedding shit on hold, or do that shit online."

I guess she took offense to me calling it 'her wedding shit', if the way she posed up like a bantam rooster was any indication. "If you don't want to go through with the wedding all you have to do is say so. I can just pack my stuff up and leave. You obviously got what you wanted and now why buy the cow when you can get the milk for free right? Jus so you know, there are more than a few men waiting to take your place." She threw the pen down on the coffee table and folded her arms like she was fucking grown. I waited until she felt the frost from my glare and looked at me.

"You on the fucking rag?" she gave me a look that I did not easily recognize, one that I did not like one fucking bit though. "Come 'ere." I grabbed her neck and turned her over the arm of the couch. "Logan quit it."

"Shut the fuck up." Just that easily she'd pissed me the fuck off. Like I didn't have enough shit to deal with she's gotta get lippy. I pulled her little flirty skirt up around her waist and tore the thong off her ass. It was no trouble getting my dick out by just pushing my jeans down around my hips.

I wasn't even gonna take the shits all the way off. That nice slow loving I'd been planning to give her for lunch was a thing of the past. I swiped my fingers through her dry pussy a couple times until she moistened up. Not her usual leaky faucet, but enough for me to get my meat in without hurting her too much.

It was a tight fucking fit and her hiss when I eased in to the hilt told me all I needed to know. "How many times I gotta tell you about your fucking mouth huh?" The 'huh' came right before a slam that sent my dick right into her deep end. I eased back and fucked into her hard over and over again, until she was babbling out an apology.

"I told you to shut the fuck up. I don't wanna hear shit." I took my dick on an adventure in her pussy, hitting places I don't think I'd ever touched before. I was aware that she was crying and telling me how sorry she was, but that shit didn't mean fuck. Her hardheaded ass needed to be taught a fucking lesson. I kept one hand in her hair and the other on her hip guiding her on and off my dick, and made each stroke count.

She tried pulling off my dick, but my hand in her hair held her in place. "The fuck you going?" I slammed into her over and over again before reaching around and teasing her clit. Just as her body started to wind up I removed my fingers from her clit, pulled out of her pussy and came in her back.

"Think about what the fuck you just said to me, and next time you won't get off so fucking easy." I left her ass crying on the couch with her skirt up around her waist and my seed running down her back. The fuck outta here! "Don't even think about leaving this fucking house." I slammed out the door done. Who the fuck was she talking to anyway?

***

I was too pissed to think straight and the others seemed to notice that when we reconvened. No one said anything to me about it until a good hour later when I'd cooled down a little. She'd tried calling me in that hour and my phone had dinged with a few texts in that time that I was sure were from her, but I ignored them. I'd had time to think while I was pissed, but not about my woman and her fucking PMS melt down.

No my mind had gone over all the things that had been going down here lately, and some things just weren't adding up. I stepped away from everything in my head for a hot minute. Things were changing for us, most of them good, some were a little fucked, but nothing we couldn't handle. I was going to be an uncle soon, that was a giant step in the right fucking direction if you ask me, and before anything else was done around here, as the designated head of our little family, I'm gonna see to it that our boy came into a peaceful world.

It didn't matter what was going on around us, we were never gonna lose sight of the greater purpose of us being here. We'd earned this little piece of heaven, and I aimed to see we got it.

"I'll be right back guys." I knew they thought I was headed back to my house to fix whatever the fuck had gone wrong between the last time they'd seen me and now, but my mind wasn't even on that shit.

Instead I called one of my contacts to see about the mission that was hanging over our heads. I needed to get that shit squared first and foremost, and was more than a little surprised by what I learned. He couldn't tell me much about something he knew nothing about, so it was a short fucking conversation. I'm not in the habit of keeping shit from my men so we had a little huddle and I conveyed what I'd learned.

"What the fuck, that doesn't make any sense. He of all people should know something about the mission." There was a heated debate about the implications of this, but the boys and I decided to shelf it for now, since there was really nothing else we could do. But it was passing strange that someone as high up in authority as he was, had no idea what I was talking about.

More alarming was the amount of time between the call-up and actual deployment; that shit's just not done. My guy on the inside didn't sound too pleased by the shit either, or the fact that he knew nothing and was only now hearing about it from me. Something was way the fuck off.

Granted it hadn't been his division that had contacted us, and sometimes these things were kept close to the vest, it was still weird that he hadn't heard a whiff of what was going on. Either the shit was more volatile than we'd first thought, or someone had got their wires crossed somewhere.

Either way it looked like we had bought some time, which with the news of Con's impending fatherhood, was most welcome. Chances are we'd end up scrapping the mission because of this turn of events. It was a hard call to make, but we worked together or not at all, and I wasn't about to take my brother into combat under these circumstances.

We'd done our bid ten times over and were free and clear. It would've been a favor in the old man's memory, but getting to the bottom of this shit now took precedence as far as I was concerned. It was more important to me to make sure our own backyard was safe than some hellhole in some remote part of the world that would

just go back to the same old same old
ten minutes after we cleared out.

While I'd been taking care of
that, each of the men were taking care
of other things, gathering more
information. We now knew that the
closest base was ten and a half miles
away, which wasn't far at all, and that
the man in charge was well known and
respected.

He ran a tight ship and was
known as a hard ass stickler for the
rules type. If this was coming out of
his house he didn't know about it, and
that was a little hard to swallow with a
reputation like his, you can't have it
both ways. But neither was I ready to
start pointing fingers at anyone.

The day dragged the fuck on
since we had nothing else to do but
wait. Vanessa was bringing in the
woman and we were all chomping at
the bit to see what if anything she
could tell us. "You need to go talk to

your girl bro, she looks miserable as fuck."
"I don't have time for this shit now Connor, I've got more important things on my mind."
"Yeah, more important than her? Look, I know they can be a trial, and heaven knows Dani knows every fucking last one of my buttons to push, but they're ours bro.

They're the best fucking things to ever happen to us in this fucked up life." Happy motherfucker, soup to nuts he'd be trying to wring Dani's neck in a day or two when she starts giving him fits again. "Ty is right, you're pussy whipped." I smirked as I walked away. Maybe he had a point.

***

I read her million and one texts on the way to the house, each of them a different variation on I'm sorry. Fucking female will drive me to drink. She was in the house curled up on the church wrapped up in a blanket like a mummy.

I wonder how Con knew she looked miserable, which she did. She probably called him over to set him on my ass which was a neat little trick she and Dani had; play monkey in the middle. I didn't say anything just stood over her until she looked up at me with red eyes, and a blotchy nose. My perfect baby, fuck.

I picked her up and sat her on my lap and not once did I complain about how fucking hot it was outside while she was wrapped up like we were in a Deepfreeze or some shit. Maybe her pussy hurt, serve her mean ass right. "Do you understand why I got so mad at you?" she nodded her head against my chest and sniffled. "You can't tell a man like me that there are other men lined up waiting for you. First thing I'll do is go find every last one of those motherfuckers and de-ball them. Then I'd skin your little ass and tie you to my bed for all time so no one else could ever get at you."

"It's not true Logan, I was just hurt because you seem to always want to put off the wedding." I held her closer because I understood how she could misinterpret shit.

I haven't been exactly forthcoming in the last few days because I don't want her stressing about this shit, but I didn't know her mind was gonna go off the fucking rails.

"Babe I'm not trying to put off the wedding, there's some things going on that me and the guys need to take care of before we can relax again. I don't want you involved so I'm not gonna tell you any more than that, just stop with the crazy okay. I want to marry you, more than anything in this world I wanna marry you, come 'ere."

I could hear Ty in my mind calling me bitch made but I didn't give a fuck.

I turned her around on my lap and fought with the blanket to get to her skin. When I had all her pertinent parts free, I fingered her pussy until she was sighing into my neck, then lifted her enough to seat her on my cock.

"I need your tit in my mouth, now." Now it was her turn to fight with her clothes to get me what I wanted. "Feed it to me." She held her tit up to my mouth as she rode my cock with my hands on her ass.

" I love the way you ride my cock, like you're enjoying the fuck out of it." And she did, all those horse-riding lessons came in handy when she got on my dick, she had great muscle control.

Her tits seemed a little fuller in my mouth; she was probably close to her period, that'll explain her attitude I guess. "Are you tender?" I hefted her tits in my hands as I pushed up into her. "Not really a little tingly but nothing bad."

I went back to mauling her flesh as she dripped all over my dick. There were no rushed movements, just a nice slow up and down, in and out that made us both happy. "I love you baby."

Her pussy tightened around me and she wept in my neck. "I love you too." I rolled my eyes where she couldn't see. Just why the fuck was she crying, who knows? I held her a little bit closer and let her tit for her lips, and when she started a nice slow cum, I bit into her neck to mark her, let her know she was mine all the way.

We ended up fucking one more time on the couch, this time I had her on her back as I drilled into her and whispered words of love and encouragement to her. I don't know why the fuck I bother going upside her damn head when she acts up, because I end up putting in more time making up for that shit in the long run; high maintenance pain in the ass.

"We straight?" I flicked off the water and stepped out of the shower where she'd just sucked the last of my energy out through my dick. She sure knew how to make it up to her man.

The sun was gonna be going down soon and then the real fun would start, our visitor was gonna be here a few hours after that. "Oh shoot, I gotta start dinner."

She slapped on her lotion and whatever the fuck else she used to make her smell fuckable before rushing out of the room. "What's the rush?" Granted after that five star breakfast I couldn't wait to scc what she could do with dinner, but she was acting like there was a fire. "I wanna cook for the guys tonight. Breakfast was such a big hit I don't feel any of my old fears anymore." Poor baby, she looked so excited I didn't have the heart to tell her that if you feed wild animals they always come begging for more. I'll just have to knock some heads together and make sure they know not to fuck with me on this shit.

She threw on jeans and a white button down top, just some shit she pulled out of the walk-in closet, but made her look like she were getting ready for a magazine shoot.

"Flawless." I like the way her eyes went all dreamy when I cupped her nape to hold her in place for a deep long kiss. "Don't overdo it okay baby, just throw some scraps on a plate, they'll appreciate it." She gave me the bitch brow and jetted. Fine, I tried. I left the house in search of the hoard of wild beast that would be descending on my home in about two hours or so. The fucking kids were still here, but there was nothing to be done about that now, at least Davey had to be here for his own protection, the sister, well, that was another story.

We ended up meeting up in the yard. No one wanted to go to the old man's place because we had all unofficially decided tot take a break since there was nothing else to be done for now.

Connor was the last to join us, I'm guessing in the next few months it's going to be like that. The decision not to go anywhere was getting easier and easier. "Listen up, Gabriella's in there making some kinda spread." The pigs started rubbing their bellies and grunting already.

That would be Ty the ringleader, Devon and Quinn. Zak just smiled and Cord was looking over at where the two kids were setting up to play ball. When is the last time any of us had used the court? It had been a while.

"I don't want you freaks overworking her with this shit, or this would be the first and the last time."

Connor had had to have this same discussion weeks ago, for all the good it did him, I figured I could at least try.

"What's she making Cap?" how the fuck should I know? "Tyler, come back here you greedy fuck. How's Dani doing bro, we need to do something special for her soon, a baby is a big fucking deal."

"Yeah it's called a shower and the women usually take care of it, bitch made." Ty shook his head while the others laughed at his antics. "Fine, but in the meantime we need to have a celebration, just a nice night out somewhere. Even though the mother to be can't drink we can still go out somewhere to celebrate the fact that we're gonna be uncles and Con's gonna be a dad. We're not gonna hide out in here from these fucks forever. We need to figure out what to do with the kid, the asshole didn't mention him when he called, let's hope he just thinks the kid missed or we got the drop on him." I looked around at each of them and everyone seemed to be in agreement.

The more I thought about it, the more it seemed the kid was just collateral damage, not really a threat. If they suspected him of talking to the commander, they had to know by now that he didn't know shit, but I didn't think so.

From what the boy had described, it seems like the old man had been very crafty in their dealings, only meeting at certain times of the day, and never being seen talking together in public.

"I say we work on getting the kids home tonight, tomorrow the latest, we've got enough to worry about without the added stress." Cord shifted from one leg to the next and I waited, but he didn't say a thing. Talk soon turned to the situation with the Desert Fox and when we all put our heads together, it really didn't make sense.

The thing about dealing with the military, unless you were the headman in charge, nothing had to make sense, you just followed orders. Our only saving grace is that we were out, and had been doing it as a favor. But there was nothing that said I had to take my men into a fucked up situation if I didn't want to. They may try to shame us, but that shit never works. We had too much to live for these days.

Chapter 14

GABRIELLA

"I'm telling you, there's something major going on, and I think it has something to do with that explosion we heard down by the water the other night." I was putting the last stir on my whipped potatoes; with one last taste on the tip of my finger it was ready.

Dani was sitting on one of the kitchen stools at the island sipping on a ginger ale; it seems her morning sickness had got its times mixed up. "Did Connor say anything to you?"

"Nope, and I would stay out of it if I were you. These guys aren't like what we're used to Gaby, Logan will go upside your damn head if you go meddling in this stuff, trust me, I know. I can't even ask Connor about what they're doing without getting a lecture and a warning. If I were you I'd forget all about it they know what they're doing." I checked on my NY strip to make sure they weren't overcooked and turned off the heat under the cast iron skillet I'd brought from home.

It was my nana's and had been in my family for generations. My Bourbon pepper cream sauce for the meat was next, the beans had already been blanched. I started to get a little nervous. "Maybe this wasn't such a good idea, maybe I should've waited." I went into panic mode I've been doing that a lot lately.

"Shush Gaby, we both know you can cook your ass off, stop worrying, did you see them at breakfast?" she rolled her eyes at me, and lifted her can to her lips. I looked down at the row of steaks on the platter that I'd covered with foil to keep the heat in and my chest got tight. This was my new family, what if they hated it, I was actually close to tears. "Dani." She must've heard the panic in my voice because she left her perch and came over to hug me. "This isn't about dinner is it hon?" I could only shake my head against her shoulder.

"It's the wedding, and everything that's going wrong, and Logan keeps getting mad at me because I can't keep my big mouth shut, and our beautiful wedding is going to be destroyed.' I said all that in one sentence and felt a little relieved to get it off my chest.

"That's it, I know what I have to do."
"Uh-oh, I know that look, that is the look that got me grounded more than once in this lifetime girlfriend, oh no." She's such a worrywart. "No-no-no, this is gonna be good I promise. Don't you want to have the wedding you've always dreamed of? And how amazingly cool is it that we've found brothers to marry and that we can have a double huh? But there's one fly in our ointment, whatever is going on

down at the boardwalk. Now if only we can take care of whatever it is."

"Gaby, if the guys can't do it what makes you think we can?" "Because the boys don't know our little town like we do, it's probably just some kids messing around.

Remember what we used to do down there when we were teens? It's the same thing; it's just that kids today are more advanced than we were. We had bonfires and firecrackers, these little delinquents probably have homemade bombs, I mean look who they've nabbed already, Davey. We both know what he and his cohorts get up to."

"I don't know, Connor seems to think there's more going on." She bit her lip but I could see her weakening, just a little more and I'd reel her in. "Yes but like I said, that's only because they don't know this town like we do. Our boys are SEALs babe, they're trained to see danger in everything, shoot Logan would childproof the house for me if he thought he could get away with it. Sometimes at night he takes me through all these scenarios of what-ifs. I now know the theory of how to get out of every sticky situation known to man.

But am I ever really gonna need them here in Briarwood? Come on. Look. It's our job to show these guys that they can take off the riot gear, that we're perfectly safe. Unless you wanna be under house arrest every time something goes wrong in a fifty mile radius."

"Fine, but we're being careful." She put her hand on her tummy and I had my first doubts. Nah, it was nothing I was sure, just Logan being overprotective as usual. If I wanted that wedding that I've had mapped out in my scrapbook since I was ten, I'm gonna have to do this. With my mind made up I went back to my sauce feeling ten pounds lighter.

***

LOGAN

"For the love of fuck, Ty chew." It was no question that dinner was huge hit, she'd really outdone herself. There wasn't an unloosened tab in the place. She had the biggest fucking smile on her face and that's all I cared about, though I could wish the wildebeest at my table had some damn manners.

"What's for dessert?" I closed my eyes and counted to ten, there's no point in trying to control his greed. She got up from the table and headed for the kitchen and I got up to go help her. "Cap sit your ass down, no hokey pokey while I'm waiting for dessert. If you're anything like Connor we'd end up waiting half an hour while you do who knows what in there, and some things just don't taste the same cold."

"Ty, learn to cook or better yet find a woman who can, that way you don't have to worry about what goes on in my kitchen." "Ooh nasty, I'm just saying."

He wasn't fazed by my tone, not even a little bit. I ignored his dumb ass and went in search of her to help. She was bending over taking something out of the oven and I eased up behind her and rubbed my dick into her ass. "Logan you'll make me drop the cobbler."

She placed the pan on the rack and turned into my arms. "They liked it Logan, they liked my food." I didn't have it in me to tell her that that bunch would eat fried sawdust, but it was good that she could actually cook or they'll talk about her, my brothers have no fucking etiquette whatsoever. "Yes baby I know."

Before she could open her mouth to prate away at me I swallowed her tongue while pressing my cock into the junction of her thighs. "Let's feed them real quick and get rid of them so I can have my dessert."

I nibbled my way to her ear and bit down gently before going back to her lips. "Logan we just did it like a few hours ago." That didn't stop her for reaching for my mouth or grinding her pussy onto my cock. "Your point?" Ty started pounding his hand on the table in the next room and started up a chant for dessert. I heard the kid start to laugh before he joined in. "I'm gonna skin him."

I helped her take the little mini crocks of the bubbly peach concoction out to the table after she'd spooned mounds of homemade whipped cream on top. My baby's a fucking gourmet, which means that while Dani's dealing with her pregnancy, my kitchen's gonna be like the fucking mess deck. By the time I got rid of them it was already getting late. I wasn't sure what the night would hold, but I knew I didn't want to face it without her sweet taste on my tongue, or the memory of her pussy wrapped around my cock.

That's how we ended up in bed with my dick in her mouth and her clit on my tongue. I had her on top of me in the sixty-nine and she was going to town on my dick. If I didn't know better id swear she wanted something from me.

I licked her clit until it was nice and plump in my mouth, then tongue fucked her until she squealed and creamed all over my face. I blew air into her pussy before opening her up with my fingers and going back in with my tongue.

When she was nice and sopping wet, I eased her head away from my dick, which made her grumble until I held her head down on the mattress while searching out her hole with my cock. "Right there." I sighed as I eased into her pussy.

It doesn't matter how many times I've had her, it's always exciting and new, that first feel of her. I gave her a variation of nice and slow and hard and rough. Each time she'd get used to one I'd switch up on her until she was screaming and tearing at the sheets.

"I wanna see you when I cum." I pulled out and flipped her onto her back, driving my dick back into her before she could even miss me.

I like this position. In this position I could take her breast in my mouth, kiss her lips and dig as deep into her pussy as I wanted, all of which I did now.

The orgasm hit me out of nowhere, an emotional cum. It was just having her under me, knowing what she meant, all of that combined to give me the sweetest cum of all. She felt my seed burst into her and that set her off so that she clenched and released around me as I emptied my nuts into her belly.

I had visions of a little me running around as I rested my still hard cock inside her walls. We'll talk about that shit later.

***

"I'm hoping she can shed some light on this shit, cause so far we're catching at our tail." Word had come in that Vanessa was on her way with the sub. The kid and his sister were still here, I knew why he was here, but there was no real reason for her to stay after she'd ascertained that her little brother was perfectly safe. I did gather though in the time that she's been here, that she is one over protective sister, who seems more like a mother to the boy than a sibling. If we weren't in the middle of this bullshit, watching her and Cord dance would've been funny as hell too. He was looking at her almost as much as she was eyeing him, but neither of them was about to let the other catch them at it.

"They're here Cap." Ty was on lookout, which means he was monitoring the street around our place. We had it under surveillance for at least a hundred feet or more in some places, which meant no one was getting close without us knowing it. I walked over to the laptop he was monitoring and looked over his shoulder as we all sat around in the commander's place, which had suddenly become headquarters.

"Is she coming in hot?" "Nope but I only see one body in the vehicle, no wait." Another little red dot showed up on the screen and all I could do was shake my head. "Let's head out, you two stay here and don't touch anything. The place is wired so we'll know if you even move out of this room." We started to head out but Cord stopped to have a word with the fire-breathing dragon.

I would love to have heard what he was saying that had her going hot and cold in one second flat. When she swung at him and he caught her arm and laughed I knew he was a goner. "What the fuck Cap?" he scowled as he almost walked into me, since I'd been standing behind him watching the byplay.

"She's not your usual type bro." "I don't know what you're talking about." Yeah that's why red was creeping up your damn neck, lying ass. "Sure you don't, just watch yourself, that one looks like she'd kill you in your sleep."
"I'm not afraid of one little girl, she's more talk than anything else." I'm not ready for this shit; he was totally fucking gone.

"She's tiny though Cord, damn." Not that my woman was any bigger, it's just that Gabriella and Dani for that matter, may not be tall, but somehow their personalities made them seem more mature, more able to handle men like us.

This one seemed to be all ballast. "And so fucking young."
"Are you trying to talk me out of something brother?" he stopped walking as the others went ahead.

"Never bro, not if she's what you want. I'm just saying that you're part ox, part elephant, and she looks like a high wind would blow her away." I had to rein it back in because if he wanted her I wasn't about to put a damper on it. It's just that I am over protective myself, and she did seem rather young for all her bravado earlier. I just don't want to see any of them hurt. I want each of us to find what I'd found with Gaby and Con had with Dani. And who knows, maybe I was making more of this than there really was, but then again I don't think so. I could almost feel that shit in the air.

Vanessa gave the signal for us to open the gate and we all stood around as it slid back to give her entrance. She stopped in the middle of us and hopped down with a big grin. It had been some time since we'd seen her, almost a year I think, if not more. However long it was, it was way too long, she was good people.

"Lieutenant." I walked over for a hug and at the last second hoped like fuck that Gaby wasn't spying on me from somewhere in the house. If there's one defect in my baby, it's her wide jealousy streak. She doesn't give a fuck who it is, and no amount of explanations work when she gets that shit in her head. "Captain, it's good to see you." I patted her back and released her before my Tasmanian devil came running to put her down. I hadn't told her too much about what was going down, just that we were expecting a visitor and I expected her to show her all the hospitality due a guest.

Gaby like I said gets her hackles up when there's a female involved, and she doesn't trust shit. I can't say as I blame her because I'm the same way with her. I trust my brothers with my life, and still if I felt one of them was getting too close to her, as innocent as it may be, I'd go for his fucking throat.

She walked around the back of the van, hitting the sides as she went. We walked around with her and stood behind her as she pulled open the double doors. All that could be seen were the two eyes opened wide in fear. Vanessa hopped up into the van and pulled Rosalind up by one of the ropes she had wrapped around her body. "Damn Lieu, what the fuck?" Ty the jackass was already sipping on a beer like he was really waiting for action.

I'd sent Zak on a chumped up mission slash errand because he was still acting like a bear with his paw caught. I don't know what it is about women that makes otherwise smart men fuck dumb. As soon as the time for her arrival drew near he started getting twitchy.

"The sub was getting on my damn nerves so I decided back here was best. I assume you wanted her here in one piece?" That's why we like Vanessa, even though she was a marine.

She'd worked with us on an Op in Kabul, that's where we'd all met. We'd seen her mettle then when she'd put her life on the line for another SEAL. That situation had worked out but it could've easily gone the other way. That was all that was needed to bond her as friend for life though, until some fuck went wrong between her and Zak.

She dropped the woman on the ground and was about to say something else when she stopped. If I hadn't been looking at her I would've missed it, damn. I literally saw the moment she sensed him.

Her whole body went loose and then tensed in a split second, she looked like a cartoon character the way she'd just shutdown in the middle of what she'd been doing. I did notice though that she didn't turn to look at him, but she knew exactly where he was.

Damn, this is going to be some shit. I hope I didn't open a can of stink because what just went through her was real fucking real. I'm gonna have to have a serious talk with my brother. I don't think he had any idea what that woman had in her for him, he couldn't have let her walk if he had. Whatever had gone down, I'm thinking she wasn't the one to call it quits. I'm gonna have to deal with his ass in the next few days while she was here, but fuck he can be a hardheaded ass, this was not going to be a walk in the park.

Looking around I realized that the others had noticed it too, and no one was making any wise cracks, in fact no one was saying anything. The only sound that could be heard was the moaning, or complaining that was coming from behind the gag that the prisoner was wearing.

I waited to see who was gonna break first, but he didn't say anything and neither did she. Now I remember why they had such a tumultuous relationship in the first place; they were both thick as fuck. I rolled my eyes and picked the woman up by her bound hands before removing her gag. She looked around in fear, because although she might not have seen us that night, she had to know that this was more of the same. Connor the fuck wanted to work her over because of what she'd tried to do to Dani, he didn't care that she wasn't sporting a dick; he just wanted answers.

Ty would slit her throat if he thought she knew who was behind it and was refusing to talk, and I'm not too sure about the others. "She's not staying in the commander's house. Tie her ass up in the yard somewhere." Damn, I hadn't even asked the question.

"Now Ty, we need to treat our guest with a little more decorum than that, this is the south after all." I didn't know where the fuck to take her but he was right, she wasn't stepping foot in the old man's place, it would be an insult. "Well she can't stay with me and I'm not sure I trust any of you with her overnight, so what do you suggest? Other than tying her up outside like a canine."

"Let's just question her first, the question of where she stays might not matter, not if we end up slitting her throat for being stupid." Fucking Connor, bastard can hold a grudge like nobody's business. Of course she opened her mouth to scream and before I could stop her Vanessa very obligingly throat punched her. "She does that a lot." She brushed off her hand while the woman gagged. I'm surrounded by fucking animals!

***

In the end we went with the old guest cottage behind the old man's place and chose Devon as night watch since he was the only one not bitching about something, though that didn't mean he was any more trustworthy. This woman's life was in danger no doubt about it. "Cord take your charges back to my place." They'd been so quiet this whole time I'd almost forgotten they were there, but I didn't need anyone in our business. They'd both been frisked and were both clean and besides, they knew the girls so there was no worry that they might try something.

Still, I called my woman with orders. "Those two kids are coming back to the house, either of them try anything aim to kill, remember to protect Dani and the baby."

"Who is she?" Dammit, I need this shit. Why would a woman who looked like Gaby, and who knew that she had her man tied all the way the fuck up in knots suffer that jealousy shit?
"Fuck babe not now, she's Zak's." Her harrumph told me she didn't give a fuck what I said and I was gonna have to deal with her shit later. She hung up on me, but at least she was in a fucked up mood, anyone tried anything she'd take 'em out. My sigh was long suffering because I truly was about at the end of my rope. Not with Gaby and her shit, but with all the up in the air

bullshit that had been going on lately. "Let's get this over with."

I led the way to the cottage that hadn't been used in over a year and had that smell of disuse about it. There were sheets over everything once we turned on the lights. "Okay, we didn't have much time last time, but we need some answers and you're gonna give them to us."

She opened her mouth to speak from her place on the dusty floor in the middle of us, but I held my hand up. "Before you open your mouth to lie I think you should know that we know a lot more than we did last time and if you bullshit me, I will let one of these fucks slit your throat since we know these guys killed our commander."

Her eyes gave her away before she opened her mouth again. "I had nothing to do with that, I was just the scapegoat for the money thing." Her eyes were even more afraid than before and I felt the shift in the room.

It was one thing to suspect and quite another to have verification.

Con moved to stand next to Tyler but I wasn't sure he was the only danger. She might not have offed the old man herself, but she was in bed with the fucks who did it. "Tell me everything you know, from the moment they contacted you, to now." She swallowed hard and looked around for an ally, there was none to be had. Right now I might be the only thing keeping her alive.

"What guarantee do I have if I talk? These people are vicious, if they even know that I'm here they'll kill me." I didn't stop Ty when he moved towards her. "What guarantee do you have that I won't cut your lying tongue from your head right fucking now?" he brandished his knife and she tried to escape through the floorboards. "Now talk bitch and make it good, I'm not like my brothers here, you're a waste of space that I won't mind offing and dumping somewhere, I give a shit that you're a chick." I gave her time to compose herself and get used to the fact that her life depended on what the fuck she said in the next five minutes.

"Okay, okay. Robert approached me, we knew each other from gambler's anonymous or one of those deadbeat things, I was so high at the time I don't remember which. I don't know, I guess in an off moment I'd actually told the truth about myself, how I had lost everything because I'd embezzled funds and the only reason I hadn't done a longer stretch is because I'd been so good at it that the feds had recruited me for a job.

But my life went into a downward spiral after that and I started using and drinking and everything in between. I don't know how Robert got in bed with those guys, he never said and we never really got into it. I just knew that they needed money moved and he knew I was good at hiding large sums of money under the radar.

Her came up with the idea of using the charity, and I kinda got the impression that everything was local, though no one ever said, just from some overheard conversations everyone seemed to know everyone. I wasn't part of the whole smuggling thing, anything I know about that is just hear say."

She looked like she was really afraid that we were gonna ask her to testify or some shit. "We're not asking you to stand up in a court of law and point fingers at anyone, just tell us what you know." No because these fucks were never gonna see the inside of a courthouse, not if I had anything to say about it.

"Yeah, okay, like I said, Robert brought me in to work the money angle, he set up the meet with his ex." Her eyes went to Connor and she lost a little color, and with good reason. "When you refer to her in the future you will use her name, it's Danielle,

the woman you had no problem setting
up for a fall is Danielle and she isn't
his ex anything."

Oh yeah, she'll be lucky if she
makes it out of here alive. "Sorry, okay
Danielle, he set it up with Danielle so
that I could get the job. I swear I
wanted to change my mind after I met
her, but you don't know these guys,
they don't care about anything or
anyone."

"Tell me about these guys." I
moved in closer, now we were getting
somewhere.
"I don't really know that much the one
time I saw one of them by mistake
they almost killed me. Robert had let it
slip that they were having some kind
of meet, not him, just the guy that's in
charge and one of the go-betweens I
guess. I got nosy, I wanted to know
who we were dealing with because that
was a lot of money and I wanted some
insurance just in case things went
south.

I was even playing around with the idea of going to the feds." Lying ass, the feds never entered your mind. Even now the signs of a true junkie were riding her hard. She was sweating from more than fear, her eyes were blood shot and her skin had that clammy unhealthy look an addict gets over time.

"This guy you saw, tell me about him."
"Uh, stocky, with a low haircut, military I think, not very tall five-nine I'd say. It was the way he walked though that stood out, and the tattoo high up on his arm." I looked at the others, sounded like the same asshole Davey had seen down by the pier.
"Go on." you could hear a pin drop in the room, no one so much as twitched as we listened to her recitation of what she had seen that night. "I remember his voice, it didn't really go with this body type, kinda girlish like but there

was nothing girlish about the way he went after me.

It was only the other guy who stopped him from snapping my neck I'm convinced, and only because he said it would be too messy."

"This other guy what did he look like?"
"That's the funny thing, I never saw him, he stayed in the shadows, but I remember the smell of his cigar it had a sweetish smell to it; and his voice, very authoritative."

She didn't remember much more after that and believed me we grilled her, if she'd had anything more we would've gotten it out of her. "Can I go now?" She looked at Vanessa who looked like she'd like nothing better than to scalp her ass. "No, you're staying here for at least tonight, we'll decide what to do with you in the morning."

"But I've told you everything I know, why do I have to stay here?" "Because you're a lying bitch who'd sell her own mother for a dollar and we don't trust your ass." I think it's safe to say Connor did not like this woman.

"I need a drink. You, stay here, I think you should know your friends are watching this place so if you try to leave they'll most likely take you out. That's if you get past our security, which I guarantee you you won't. Put her out."

She held up her hands when Devon moved towards her with the needle. That ought to knock her out for the next eight hours or so. I ended up having to drag her to the couch myself since no one else was willing to, before we headed out the door.

"Let's get the women and go have some fun, I need it after this shit, and we're supposed to be celebrating, fuck this." I checked my watch, it was getting late but the little spot we'd found in the next town over didn't close until about three or four so we were good, unless the girls were tired.

"Cord you cool with us dropping the kids off?" he had to think about it which told me more than words where we were at. "They're safe enough, I didn't pick up anything when I did a run through, but I think we should keep an eye out for the next few days just in case."
"Fair enough."

Chapter 15

LOGAN

For some fucked up reason the kids didn't wanna leave, the female especially seemed the most reluctant though she tried to play it off. I noticed she was no longer breathing fire, she seemed calm as fuck compared to when she first arrived and I wondered what the fuck Cord had said or done to her in the past few hours to tame that beast.

I introduced Gabriella to Vanessa, which helped to calm her ass down a little, but she still clung to my arm like she was marking her territory. Even though we'd checked and double- checked the area, we were still careful as we headed out of town. We rode in three vans funnily enough with three couples in one and then two and two in front and behind for security. Zak and Vanessa still hadn't said fuck all to each other but I noticed that he'd been quick to jump in the truck with her when she followed the girls.

The night was the usual balmy clear skies with a nice breeze and the women were acting more excited than the rest of us, like we'd held them prisoner for a month instead of a couple of days.

Vanessa was involved in the conversation like the three of them had known each other since birth, especially when it came to talk of the baby. I watched Zak in the rearview and that fucker was hanging onto every word.

"Hey Lieu if I didn't know better I'd think you've done this before." She stopped in the middle of her sentence and looked around like Bambi caught in the headlights. What the fuck was that about?

"No captain, just my experience from being around my sisters and cousins with their pregnancies." Zak looked at her like he wanted to fall on her in the back of my damn truck but I didn't say a word, whatever he had brewing I was pretty sure it wouldn't be long before it came bubbling to the top.

We reached the bar and it looked like the place was still hopping, the weekend was just getting started so that could be the reason for the overflowing parking lot.

We hadn't been here since the night I'd snagged Gabriella in fact it was the first time we'd really been anywhere in quite a while. "Okay crew, you know the deal, have fun and we'll pick shit up tomorrow." The ten of us headed in the doors and straight for the tables in the corner. Con and I pushed a couple together with our backs to the wall and a clear view of the door, which is our usual. The bartender hailed us and without being told started lining off our drinks of choice.

Ty stayed at the bar for now and I let him because I knew he was working through some shit, so I took off my captain's cap and put on the fiancé cape.

Con and Dani were already off in a corner smooching and pretending to dance and Gabriella was smiling, that's all the fuck I cared about. I saw the little one that was on Ty's dick walk in not long after and looked at my sneak.

"What did you do?" She gave me the 'who me' innocent bullshit look but I wasn't buying it, especially when she raised her hand and beckoned her over. Dammit, why arc these women always playing an angle, and when the fuck did she have time to call her between the time I'd told her to get dressed and the time we left the house? Fucking women.

I looked over at Ty and wondered if I'd had the same reaction to Gabriella, as he and Vanessa seemed to have to their mate. I was pretty sure he knew the second she walked in. Some strange shit has been going on since we came to this town. If I didn't know better I'd swear the old man was up there playing matchmaker or some shit.

***

TYLER

I don't know why she does it to me but she does. If I see her hear her or smell her, I'm transported to another place, another time and I'm not myself. It's almost as if she's haunting me with her very existence and I can't shake it off. Sitting at the bar with a couple of my brothers throwing back a

few, trying to unwind from the fucked
up day we'd had she walks right in.

I didn't have to turn around to
know that it was her, every hair on my
body stood on end and my cock started
throbbing, that was always the way,
even if I didn't see her, just from my
body's reaction alone I always knew.
My own personal alarm!

Her voice reached my ears as she
greeted one of her friends, I knew how
this was going to play out, she'll
pretend that I wasn't here she'll say
hello to my brothers and sisters and
pointedly ignore me. Maybe I
should've taken her up on her
unspoken offer a few weeks ago, but I
wasn't ready for her kind of fun. She's
the marrying kind and I'm just not
ready to slip on the noose. And at the
rate these fuckers were dropping, I
knew if I even entertained the thought
I'd be a goner. I wasn't blind. I'd seen
the way Cord reacted to that Susie girl
who if you asked me was a candidate
for a lobotomy.

Yes Vitoria Lynn was hot, she was sweet as fuck too from what I'd seen, but she wasn't for me, too fucking innocent. Besides she was a tiny little thing, which seems to be the only thing this town produces. Then again Nessa wasn't from here and she wasn't that much taller than the others come to think of it. Maybe that's just the type of woman we attract; the dainty kind that looked like a hard fuck would break them in half.

I watched her out of the corner of my eye as she flirted her way across the room. Every guy had his eye on her whether he was alone or with someone, she just had that kind of effect on the male of the species. That was another reason for me to steer clear. I'm a hotheaded bastard, I know that better than anyone else and if she ever fucked around and flirted with some other man I might snap and do her harm, so it was best for all concerned if I just stayed the fuck away from one Victoria Lynn Delaney.

I could see my brothers watching me covertly but when you've spent the last ten years or so in very close proximity to men in tight quarters you get to know them so they weren't fooling me one bit. Logan left where he was with his nosy ass and made his way over to the bar where Devon and Quinn had been keeping me company.

"Kill it boys."
"What Tyler?"
Logan was always the ringleader always the one pushing.
"I'm not going there okay so kill it."
My brother Connor and his woman were in the corner smooching as usual so I had two less nosy fuckers to contend with. My new little sister Danielle is relentless, she couldn't understand why I wouldn't give her friend a chance. She believed that since she had my brother wrapped around her finger that it was only a matter of time before the rest of us fell.

Now there was Gabriella and she was giving me looks, fucking set me up.

I was listening to them but my attention was completely on her as she made her way to the table where Gaby and Nessa were sitting talking. Zak was on the wall not too far away pretending not to be watching Nessa and I felt the noose tightening around my neck.

"Just what the fuck is it about this town?" I didn't have to expound, they knew exactly what I was talking about.
"I don't know brother, but I can tell you, it doesn't pay to fight it, just go with the flow, it's a lot easier. Logan the pussy whipped was full of advice but I seem to remember a time when he was singing a different tune.

LOGAN

The night wasn't turning out to be half bad. Everyone seemed to be having a good time except Ty who seemed to be grumbling in his beer. He had his eye on Vicky the whole time even though he was slick about it, and thank fuck she had ignored my little upstart's suggestion that she dance with the next man who asked her to. I wasn't trying to get kicked out of the only decent watering hole in a ten-mile radius.

So it didn't look like Ty was gonna fold tonight but there was still a lot of fodder for my shits and giggles. Like Dani trying to convince Con that it was oaky for her to have a half a glass of wine, and him having a conniption, funny shit. Or the way Cord was mooning into his mug, like he'd lost his best friend, good times.

"It's already late." What the fuck? Vanessa's raised voice came out of left field.

"I said you're not going and that's final."

"Who made you the boss of me Zachary? I can go where I want when I want and with whom I want."

"Try that shit and it'll end bad for you swear to fuck."

"Alright you two break it up." Fuck Ty was right, it was like watching the Tyson Holyfield bout all over again in techni-fucking-color. "What seems to be the problem?"

"She thinks she's heading into the next town over to find a place to stay, and this asshole's been sniffing around her all fucking night." He glowered at some poor smuck across the room who probably had no idea that his life span was now being counted in minutes. I need this shit.

"I am going to find a place to stay and you can't stop me." Well now, she wasn't backing down and I know for a fact that he won't so we're in a pickle. Just once I could wish for a female who wasn't so damn fearless and ballsy, it's like our size didn't matter, they all still think they can take us on.

"Uh Vanessa he has a point. We have more than enough room at the compound. You can stay with Gaby and me or Con and Dani or…"
"She's fucking staying with me." Okay cowboy who's arguing? Damn.
"I am not." When he stepped into her like he was giving serious thought to popping her one I figured I'd better intervene.

"Okay, listen, we can't do this here first of all, and second, Nessa, none of us are gonna let you go off on your own. Let's get back to the compound and the question of where you spend the night can be solved there."
She didn't agree with it I could tell, but she caved because I'm pretty sure she

knew Zak didn't have any give in him worth a damn.

We headed back to the compound feeling a lot lighter than when we left and I just wanted my bed. Tomorrow promised to be another trying day because we still weren't any closer to figuring this shit out and I couldn't shake the feeling that we were racing against the clock.

We ended up having to drop Ty's future whatever home because she'd taken a cab there at my woman's suggestion, sneaky fuck. I wasn't really worried about where Vanessa slept as long as it was within these gates, so as soon as we were all safe inside I left the rest of them to their shit.

Ty was still griping about being cornered, but I knew what his problem was. Somebody had given his little filly pointers and she wasn't putting up with his shit. The two of them had

played the ignore game all night until
it was time to leave, and the way she
spoke to him there at the end,
permafrost.

I dragged my pain in the ass off
to bed and left the rest of them to their
own recognizance, tomorrow was soon
enough to deal with their brand of
fuckery.

Vanessa cussed out Zak at the
top of her lungs as he dragged her ass
off to his lair, to the entertainment of
Ty who was over his snit it seemed. I
heard one last complaint for the night,
this time from Devon who was
supposed to be watching over our
guest for the night.

"Babe, what the fuck have you
been telling that girl?"
"What girl?" She wanted to play
dumb.
"You wanna play dumb fine, but when
she pushes Ty too far I hope you're
willing to bear the consequences."
That seemed to put a little hitch in her

giddy-up. "What do you mean, he wouldn't really hurt her would he?" it would serve her right if I left her with that impression in mind, but I couldn't do that to my brother.

"No, but if you push him into a corner you might not like the results. And for fuck sake don't tell her about flirting with other guys, you trying to get her ass killed?" now she was back to worrying, good, maybe now she'd stay her nosy ass out of other people's shit.

"I don't see what's the big deal. You gave me a hard time now look at you." She got jokes. I got sidetracked when she pulled her jeans down and off. "What's that you got there?" she had some kind of gem hanging from her clit.
"Oh Dani and I were bored waiting around so we pierced each other's clits."
"You did what?"

"It's a joke, it's just a clip on." I grinned because I could already imagine the fun we were gonna have with that.

"Leave it on." we both rushed onto the bed and I rummaged around in the nightstand for some goodies. I got out the ben-wa balls and some lube.

"Open." She spread her legs for my mouth and I climbed in between them to warm her up. I used my tongue to get her off and just as she was cresting, I slipped the balls inside her, using my finger to push them as far up in her as they would go.

Next I teased the little diamond in her clit with my tongue while shoving my thumb in her ass. She was in heaven. She started fucking my face even before I got started on her pussy.

I went in search of the beads with my tongue but they were too far, so I satisfied myself with eating her out until she came in my mouth. I nibbled her flesh as she wound down, leaving my mark on her thigh her hips and her tummy, making my way up to her tits. I slipped my cock into her as I took her nipple into my mouth, and felt the balls rolling around in there at the tip of my cockhead.

"Oh Logan that feels so nice." I went deep on each stroke, knocking the balls together inside her. She was juicing all over my dick and tearing the skin from my back in her lust craze.

I wasn't even doing her hard, I didn't need to, the added sensation of the beads and the ring in her clit had her continuously cumming on my dick, who was as happy as he'd ever been.

"Raise your legs up here." She wasn't paying me any mind so I lifted her legs myself and held them open and high at an angle so I could fuck into her however I wanted. Her eyes rolled back in her head when one of my strokes went too deep and her body started to convulse. "Oh shit, oh fuck." I tried to pull out but her body went into some sort of lockdown and trapped my dick inside. Her pussy quivered as she jerked and the movement had me spewing a jet stream of cum inside her that seemed like it would never end.

"Baby, talk to me, come on." She was out of it and I still had to wait for her body to relax to pull out. I ran into the bathroom for a wet cloth and tried to bring her back that way. Her breathing was normal and her pulse wasn't accelerated, and it took me a minute to figure out that she'd fainted. I didn't know what the fuck to do, should I touch her, try to wake her what?

She came to five minutes later, the longest fucking five minutes of my life. I started to pull the beads out and her body did that shit again and scared the fuck outta me. She stayed awake this time thank fuck but I'm thinking that's it for the beads.

"What the fuck happened? my heart was in my lungs and this one was grinning like a Cheshire cat. "Oh Logan it was amazing, we have so got to that again." Not in this fucking lifetime.

She stretched and reached out for me, which meant her pussy was still hungry. My boy had gone into hiding because he thought he was in trouble. "Since you scared the fuck out of him, you get him back up." She rolled into me with a nasty smile on her face; fuck I forgot her and alcohol, oh well.

"No problem honey bear." I just rolled my eyes at her drunk ass and let her do her thing. When she licked my dick down to the nuts with her juices and mine still on it, I knew what kinda mood she was in.

She likes when I kneel over her with my dick in her face while she reclines against the pillows. I fed her my cock little by little until she had a mouthful, then I fucked into her throat slowly. I held her head in my hands and throat fucked her until she gagged with pre-cum running down her chin. I wasn't going anywhere near her pussy again with my dick, so I used my fingers to get her off while she sucked the skin of my dick.

When my dick started to jump on her tongue and her pussy tightened around my fingers I pulled out of her throat and sprayed all over her tits. All in all it was a good night.

Chapter 16

GABRIELLA

"So here's the deal, we have got to find out what's going on down by the water. So far we know squat and this affects our lives as well." Dani and I and our new friend Vanessa were sitting around drinking coffee while the men folk were out and about doing who knows what.

"I don't think that's such a good idea, and whatever you're gonna do I can't know about it because I ought to know better."
"Oh come on Vanessa, you're like one of them if you go with, you can be our protection. Besides, we're not doing anything, just going to see what they missed."

Dani wasn't looking too sure either but I knew how to bring her around. I had to work on this Vanessa person because Logan had left her here with us, knowing him she was supposed to be more watchman than pal, but later for that. I have a wedding coming up in a few short months and all this cops and robbers mess was interfering with my program. "They don't even have to know we went anywhere.

They left on an errand didn't they? It's just a quick trip to the pier and back." I'd dragged as much information out of Davey yesterday that I could and knew that something had gone down but he wasn't saying what.

I did garner that the guys had been down there looking for something, I just don't know what, and now they had that awful woman that used to work for Dani locked away in the cottage. Since no one was talking I figured it was up to us women to figure out just what in the Sam hill was going on; and with Vanessa being G.I Jane and all, why not?"

"Gaby I'm with Vanessa, we don't know what all is going on down there, I think we should leave well enough alone." she's just afraid of Connor, but who wouldn't be? I wasn't even gonna think about Logan's reaction if he found out about my little side trip, but he wasn't gonna find out because we were gonna be gone and back before he came home.

"Fine, if you two won't go with me I'll do it by myself, but I bet you there's nothing going on down there but a bunch of kids acting the fool." I just wanted to go and catch them in the act so that we could put this whole mess behind us and move on.

I'm sure if I had the proof that there was nothing really going on that Logan would settle down and help me plan the wedding.

I got up from my chair and headed for the closet to get my shoes. The sun had been down for a few hours and it was almost full dark. Logan and the guys had gone somewhere to check out something and he said they wouldn't be back for a couple hours at least.

The woman was under lock and key and no one said anything about us having to watch her. I figured if I made the move to go, that these two would follow. "Let it be noted that I'm doing this under duress."

"Yeah, I knew I was gonna like you Vanessa." Dani was still looking doubtful but I knew she wasn't gonna want to be left out, and I was right. "Your ass is still getting me into trouble, I'm telling you, these men have radar. They're gonna know the second we leave the compound."

"You need to stop watching Sci-Fi, now come along." I took her hand and pulled her along before she chickened out. I had a moment's pause when I remembered the baby, but soon squashed it. I'm sure I was right, there was nothing to worry about.

***

LOGAN

"What the fuck?"
"What is it?" Connor reacted to the tone of my voice, and the others raised their heads from their positions in the brush, surrounding the place we were told we might be able to find the man that fit the description we'd received from both Rosalind and Davey.

"Check your watch Con." I didn't even need to explain as he looked at his and had the same reaction, before we were both heading for our rides. My mind went into combat mode as the others fell in behind us.

"What's going on?" Ty was the first to catch up with us.
"The girls are on the move." That sent everyone scrambling for their bikes as a thousand scenarios went through my head.

It wasn't a breech because each of us had a special alarm on our phones that would've gone off if someone had got past the perimeter, so where the fuck were they going? Had someone tricked them into leaving? It's the only thing I could figure since I'd told Gabriella not to leave the house.

I couldn't afford to let anger, or fear, rule me now, not until I had eyes on her and knew that she was safe. After that, she'd better have a good fucking excuse for what she was doing away from where the fuck I'd left her.

"They're heading for the water."
Yeah, like my shit wasn't already

twisted enough, Quinn's words had me fighting to rein it in. We weren't too far out, maybe a half an hour, but every second felt like torture.

Quinn and Dev were keeping us up to date from the van as they followed behind. "Shit Lo we've got to move, they're on the run." Quinn's voice in my ear was like a dagger to the heart and we were still ten minutes away.

"Is Vanessa with them?" That was Zak, I knew he knew we had no way of knowing since we hadn't tagged her, but chances are she was, since we'd left the three of them together. I started praying as we sped through the night. No one said anything as we waited for updates from the van.

We came in sight of the pier or what was left of it just as a scream rang out and carried on the wind. Two figures were running on the beach in the dark, two men were after them, and two other figures seemed to be locked in combat. I jumped off my bike while it was still in motion and ran towards the two in front, while Zak headed for Vanessa who we rightly assumed was the one doing the fighting. Connor bypassed both of us and was on one of the assholes while the other grabbed Gabriella and put a gun to her fucking head.

I stopped short with my hands raised as chaos ensued. The others came up behind us. "Everybody stay where you are." He was desperate and a desperate man is a dangerous fucker.

His eyes were going all over the place like a cornered rat. I'd seen that look a time or two. Usually before some asshole did something stupid that got him dead. I wasn't too fond of the idea of Gaby seeing me in action, women tend to get squeamish about that shit.

"Okay, no one's gonna do anything. I won't ask you to let her go because she's your only bargaining chip, but I will ask you to think. There's only one way you're gonna survive this." I didn't look at her, couldn't. Con had the other asshole subdued and had passed Dani off to the others, while Zak had taken over kicking ass from Vanessa.

"As I was saying." I brought my attention back to him. "You kill her, I break your fucking neck, you die. You let her go I give you my word I'll let you live, after we have a little discussion about you putting a gun to my fucking woman's head. Before you give me your answer, I suggest you do a head count. Right now one of my brothers has a scope centered on your forehead." He looked around in a panic.

"Shh shh, don't do that, he might get twitchy fingers and shoot, and I really don't want your brain and shit all over my woman, so let's keep a cool head here." By then Con and Zak were bringing their guys into the circle.

A quick glance showed me that none of them were the one we were looking for, but they were definitely military, the hair, the build, the carriage; all dead giveaways. I looked back at my quarry who was sweating profusely and not looking too sure of himself. She was crying and shaking but I couldn't take that shit in right now, I had to save her life so I could wring her fucking neck for being stupid.

"Give me my woman." He looked around at all of us, and his two mates who were beat to fuck.
"No, everybody back off." He started backing up in a panic.
"Don't do tha…well fuck." She screamed loud and hard when the blood sprayed all over her face.

Cord had gone for the hand with the gun instead of the head, which was just as well because I wasn't sure how we would've explained that fuckery. I didn't go near her right away because now that the adrenaline was kicking I was beyond pissed.

The asshole was writhing on the ground holding his wrist but I left him to the others. Connor was consoling Dani and Zak was reading Vanessa the riot act. I moved towards her, not sure what I was gonna do, I couldn't even see through the haze that was over my eyes.

"Logan." She called out to me with a fearful voice but I wasn't hearing shit. I was about to tear her little ass up for putting herself in danger. I made some kind of move towards her but a fucking tank got in my way. Connor, fucker knocked me on my ass.

"Stay down Cap, you've gone FUBAR." He stood over me looking down as the others came to join him. "Yeah Cap, you stay your ass where you are."

Ty was looking down at me with a look of worry on his face. I'd only seen my brothers react this way once, when I'd lost someone on the battlefield and had lost my shit. What the fuck happened? It was as if my mind had taken flight or some shit. I looked around me not sure of what the fuck and it all came back. I had been about to strangle Gabriella's little ass.

I took a deep breath and closed my eyes, willing my heart to come back into my chest.
"Ty get your damn foot off my chest you ass." The danger had past. She was still in trouble but not as bad. Zak was shooting daggers at Vanessa with his eyes and I wasn't sure she wasn't in danger too.

"Come on let me up, I'm not gonna hurt her." I could hear her crying and it tore at my heart but I wasn't about to fall for that shit. Fucking infuriating female.

"You sure you cool?" I just nodded my head as they stepped back. I must've really been out of my shit because I don't even remember anything before feeling Con take me down.

"Con how's Dani, the baby?" I stood to my feet and dust the sand off me.
"They're fine, she just has a stitch in her side. I'm gonna run her into the emergency room as soon as I'm sure you're not gonna do anything stupid."

"I'm cool brother let's get your girl looked at. We'll keep these three on ice." Devon and Quinn had already taken them to the van and Cord had come down from his hiding place. I realized I hadn't even needed to tell my team where to go or what to do, we'd all just fallen back in the way we do.

Half of us followed Con and his woman to the hospital while the others went to stash our prisoners, who were in deep shit because they were about to miss curfew. Too bad for their asses, right now they had bigger worries.

***

Dani got the all clear and I commended Connor for his restraint. I could see he wanted to tear into her, but she'd had enough of a scare for one night so he was taking it easy. My pain in the ass however was not about to get off so easy.

I had already dragged the story out of Vanessa who had come to the hospital, and since she was feeling guilty, she shared it all. I should've known mine was the ringleader, that she was the one who'd talked the other two into this fuckery.

She was way too quiet and that could be because I was ignoring her. I'd put her in the van instead of on the back of my bike and I knew that had to sting, but I was too pissed. She tried approaching me at the hospital but I ignored her ass. The second time she got too close I leaned over and whispered in her ear.

"Stay the fuck away from me, I'll deal with you later." That really threw her ass in a tizzy. She could've been killed could've gotten others killed, like what the fuck.

We left the hospital and headed for home. I don't know what the fuck was going on, but Zak dragged Vanessa's ass off as soon as we got back to the compound. I didn't even try to intervene and neither did any of the others.

We were all just happy that they were okay. I stood around long enough to be sure Zak wasn't gonna lose control, because when that fucker goes quiet, it usually means trouble. It took me a while to figure out he was fucking her and not killing her five seconds after the door closed behind them. "Alright come on you pervs break it up." The others were just hanging around in the yard listening to shit like they were at the movies. I shook my head as I walked away.

"You know, the rest of us didn't sign on for Family Ties, this was supposed to be a bachelor compound. In less than a year you three weak fucks have gone AWOL for pussy and fucked everyone else's shit up."

Ty was in bitch mode again. He sounded grumpy and it wasn't hard to figure out what his problem was; fucker was running scared from the little beauty down at the diner.

I could tell him there was no sense in running. There was some shit in the water here in Briarwood that was designed just for us, or so it seemed. There was no other explanation for it. Sometimes I think the commander knew what he was up to when he left his boys this place. The way we were pairing off one after the other with our soul mates was something beyond. Still, can't have the boy raining on our parade.

"Ty go get your ass laid and stop being a pest." I went in search of my own woman; it was time to work off some of this anger between her thighs. Her pussy stayed on the injured list these days. Her hardheaded ass didn't seem in any hurry to learn any lesson I sought to teach her.

Now she'd fucked up but good. After tonight, she'll learn not to disobey me again. I still had to go deal with the three assholes on ice, but first things first. "Don't hide little girl get your ass out here." I knew her game as soon as I got through the door.

The lights were off and the place was still, too fucking quiet, like there wasn't another breathing soul here. That's some shit she used to do as a kid to hide from her folks when she was in trouble. Maybe if they'd spanked her ass instead of fucking timeouts I wouldn't have to deal with her shit on a bi-daily basis. I had less stressful days in the Navy for fuck sake.

I got my belt and went in search of her ass when she didn't show. I wasn't quiet when I opened the million and one doors in the place, or when I walked through the closets. I must've known I was gonna end up with a princess, because what the fuck did I need with walk-in closets as big as the damn bedrooms? "Gabriella, front and center, now." Not even a peep. It took me damn near ten minutes to find her.

Her ass was in a cubicle in my closet. "Get outta there." I snapped the belt that I had folded in half. Her eyes were glued to the leather and she wasn't looking like she was about to climb outta there anytime soon.

"Did you hear me?" she opened her mouth about to scream. "You do that shit it'll only go worse for you, now get your bad ass out here and take your licks. You wanna do the crime, do the fucking time. How many times must I tell you? If you're not willing to bear the consequences, don't do the shit that's gonna get your ass beat."

"But we were only trying to help."
"Yeah, and whose idea was that?" Her guilty look as she crawled out of the space was answer enough. "Uh-huh, you just cost your friend an ass whipping cause I'm sure as shit Connor's just as pissed off as I am. Do you know why I tell you not to do the things I tell you not to?" I pulled her along behind me to the bed.

She was already sniffling but her ass didn't get anything to sniff about yet. I sat down and pulled her down across my lap hard. "I asked you a damn question answer me." She tried picking her head up but I pushed it back down before stripping her jeans halfway down her thighs. "For my own good, to protect me." Now she wants to sulk.

"So what the fuck were you doing down there?" I brought the belt down across her ass before she could answer me. "No Logan, no." I wailed her little ass until it went red. "Move your damn hand."

All the fear came rushing back, seeing them down there unprotected, knowing we were dealing with something very sinister but still having no clue as to what the fuck. How could she do this shit to me? If I live to be a hundred I'll never be as scared as I was tonight. Seeing that fucker with a gun to her head will haunt me for many nights to come.

"If you ever do anything like this again I won't only beat your ass I'll take you back to your father's house." I didn't realize I was this fucking pissed until I got my hands on her. I'd stopped spanking her ass long enough to talk so that she might hear me this time. "I can't have that shit in my life. My life is about order, structure. There's shit in the world that my woman have no right being a part of, if I tell your ass to stay out of something you stay the fuck out." I sat her up on her sore ass and left the room.

"Logan." She beat tracks running after me until she caught up with me at the door. Her face was a mix of terror and despair and tugged at my heartstrings.

I felt like a fucking ogre and she's the one who fucked up. Looking down at her, one thought ran through my mind. "We're not having any fucking daughters." That brought her up short. "What?" Like I'm telling her shit. That look had just shown me what a little girl made from her and me would do to me, fuck no.

She rubbed at her ass and pouted, how the fuck was she supposed to learn shit if I kept melting like putty in her hands? "I'm pissed at you, don't give me that look." She snuggled into me with her sneaky ass and all I could do was sigh and wrap my arms around her.

"You have to listen baby, there's no negotiating that shit, you fuck up again like this we're done." Yeah right you fucking sap, you wouldn't make it one day without her under your ass. But she didn't need to know that shit.

She seemed to believe me because she held on tighter and soaked my damn Henley with her shit. I held her while she cried and blubbered an apology into my chest. "But Logan it's not fair, you get to put yourself in danger but you won't let me help you."

I rolled my eyes before pushing her away so that I could look down at her.

"Were you born with a dick?" She shook her head no. "Thank fuck or I'd have to kill your ass and bury you out back. Listen up, you're a girl, you're my girl, you don't protect me from shit, I protect you. Your mom rules your dad like a fucking third world dictator, that shit's not gonna happen here, ever.

I make the rules, I do the protecting and all the other shit my nuts have ordained to be my job as a man. Now stop the bullshit and just do what the fuck I say from now on, and don't forget, no fucking female offspring."

"I'm pretty sure that's on you." I looked down at my dick, which was now pressing against my fly. "You hear that buddy? It's up to us, no girls." She cleared her throat and gave me a look that I did not trust. "What?"

She hugged me tighter and shook her head. "I can't tell you yet, I'm not sure yet." I'm fucked if I understand any of that shit.

"What are you not telling me?" I held her face up by her chin so I could read her eyes. She wasn't sad I could tell that much, but there was something going on there. "I'm pregnant." What the fuck? I think things went dark for a minute or two before life came back into focus.

"You...you're pregnant, and you went running around down there tonight?" She wasn't expecting that shit. I think I was just trying to buy time, to process the shit she'd just told me.

I didn't know what to do next. I wanted to call the boys together to tell them about my son, I wanted to take her back in the room and fuck her or maybe not fuck but make love to her. I didn't know I was going to be this happy at hearing those words. Never knew there was more joy to be had other than winning her for myself.

Dropping to my knees I laid my palm over her flat tummy. "Shit baby, he's in there?" Fuck had I hurt him when I spanked her ass? "We have to go to the doctor." I started dragging her towards the door. It didn't register that it was late at night and the doc's office was closed. We could always go back to the emergency room. "What why? I have an appointment next week."

"What if I hurt him just now?" She smiled and caressed my cheek like I was the village idiot. "You didn't, I kept him protected the whole time I was over your lap." She's doing a lot of fucking protecting around here lately.

Epilogue

LOGAN

"Unghh." I love the way she grunts when I pound her. She gripped the sheets so hard I thought they'd rip, but I didn't stop battering her pussy with my steel hard cock. Her legs shook and almost gave out on her when I changed up and went in on an angle.

"Mine…mine…mine." Oh yeah, it was one of those moments. That shit came out of nowhere and hit me like a freight train. Next thing I knew I was biting into her neck like a wolf with his mate, marking her on the outside as I scalded her pussy inside with hot jizz.

Ever since she'd told me about the baby I've been hard. Each time I think I'm done with her, my dick stands up and I have to fuck her again, it's some kind of phenomenon. I dropped down on the bed beside her, puffing like a steam engine coming into the station.

"Your pussy is gonna be the death of me." She crawled onto my chest and I held her close and kissed her hair.
"You still mad?"
"Yes." She didn't say anything for a long time. "I'm sorry Logan I won't ever be that stupid again I promise, I learned my lesson."

She's so full of shit. I've come to accept that Gabriella is always gonna be in shit, she's a magnet and that's all there is to it. I'm just gonna have to keep my eye on her for the next seventy years or so, and heaven help me, any kids we share. I placed my hand over her flat stomach and some of my anger and fear drifted away. A baby, fuck me, there really is something in the water.

"I gotta go tell the guys." I jumped off the bed and grabbed my phone while she lounged back on the bed. I took enough time to grab a quick shower before heading out after calling them for a meet. We still had to deal with the assholes before the night was done, and I had a feeling that shit had just heated up.

"What's the big emergency Cap? Some of us need to unwind after the shit your woman put us through." Ty was gnawing on some type of meat bone as we waited for the others to join us. Con came next and we watched him say bye to Dani in the doorway before coming over.

At least she didn't look any worse for wear and I could only surmise that he was taking it easy because of his son.

The others soon came, all except Zak who was probably still in his woman.

"Gaby's pregnant." I didn't bother leading up to the shit, why bother? It took a minute for it to sink in but when it did, the air shifted around us. Everyone was excited and the news went a long way to alleviating the stress of what we'd dealt with in the last few hours.

Ty of course had to make his feelings known. "It's got to be the fucking water, either that or the shit's catching." The idiot started backing away like we had the plague.

I smirked at him because from what I saw last night his time was just about up. I watched him the whole night as he pretended not to be watching Vicky, but I wasn't about to say anything because knowing his hardheaded ass, he'd deny her just for that shit.

Zak finally came waltzing out his door, but for a man who'd been busy, doing what he'd been doing, he sure didn't look rested. "What the fuck is wrong with females?" Uh-oh. He didn't even stop to find out what was going on, but kept going towards the cottage where we'd stashed the three idiots in a separate room away from the woman.

"Damn another bitch made fucker."

"Tyler would you shut the fuck up?"

THE END

***

You may find the author

https://www.facebook.com/MrsJordan Silver

Book list

http://www.amazon.com/-/e/B00C65VXJY

Mailing list

http://eepurl.com/ZGuvT

Blog

http://jordansilver.net

Twitter

https://twitter.com/JordanSilver144